DEADLY INTENT

VANISHING RANCH
BOOK 4

CHRISTY BARRITT

CHAPTER
ONE

SARAH COULDN'T DO it again.

The thought of facing Bryce Daniels made her entire body tremble uncontrollably. Made sweat break out across her skin. Made nausea churn in her stomach.

He was closing in.

She sensed it.

Sensed that someone had been in her house. That someone was watching her.

She'd escaped from the man once, but she knew better than to think she'd be lucky enough to escape again.

Dread pounded inside her as she glanced outside. She'd made a nice life here for herself in the Flathead Valley area of Montana over the past two years. For a brief period of time, Sarah had hoped this place could be permanent. That maybe she could actually continue this new life.

But now she knew that wasn't the case.

She pulled her sweater closer around her as she stepped out her back door and into the brisk early October air.

As her bare feet hit the splintery wooden deck, she glanced around.

Darkness had fallen, and the woods stood proudly around her. The moonlight shone brightly tonight, casting a silver lining on everything it touched. An owl hooted in the distance, and a clean evergreen scent filled the air.

Sarah wasn't sure exactly what she was doing. Her pulse pounded out of control. Her mind raced. Her senses felt vibrant while her mind felt scrambled.

Despite that, she took a step forward. Then another one. Then another.

She kept moving. Kept walking.

Off her deck and onto the gravel walkway snaking through the grass and leading away from her house.

She expected to feel eyes on her. To hear a footstep.

But she felt no sense of someone watching her. Heard nothing but nature around her.

Even worse, part of her didn't care if someone was watching her or not.

Fear had set in. But it wasn't a frantic fear. It was a numbing fear, one that made her feel like nothing mattered anymore.

She was so tired of fighting. *So*, so tired.

Her feet kept leading her.

On a conscious level, she wasn't sure where she was going. But subconsciously? Her scrambled thoughts led her toward the lake behind her house.

The property where she lived was located on four acres beside a gorgeous lake that backed up to the beautiful mountains. Sarah found immense comfort in looking at them every morning and delighting in how stunning this plot of land was.

She didn't want to leave. Didn't want to give up hope.

Despite that, she kept walking, her bare feet pressing into the gravel. The rocks didn't hurt. At least, if they did, she wasn't aware of it. Not yet.

Keeping a steady pace, her feet eventually hit the water lapping onto the rocky shore. The lake was cold. It was *always* cold. Some people were crazy enough to swim in it despite that.

Sarah had never been one of them.

Feeling almost as if she were in a trance, she kept walking.

The bottom of the lake dropped slightly, and the water was suddenly up to her knees.

Another few feet, and the water reached her waist.

She took several more steps, the depth remaining the same.

Then suddenly she was chest-deep.

At any minute, she could be over her head.

Then what would she do? Swim? Turn back?

Sarah wasn't sure. All logic left her. All control of her motions were gone.

Her steps slowed, and she paused a moment.

Her feet and hands tingled. Numbness was setting in. Her teeth chattered as her body fought to keep her warm.

Yet, inside, she hardly felt anything except numbness, apathy, and confusion.

Should she dive beneath the water and take a swim? See what happened?

Or should she turn around and go back to the little house she called home, hoping and praying for the best? Hoping and praying that Bryce's hands didn't find their way around her neck again?

Tears pressed at her eyes.

Sarah stood in the water another moment, looking at the serene lake and contemplating her actions.

Then she took another step.

Ruger pulled to a stop at the small, wooded cottage, cut his engine, grabbed his duffle bag, and quietly stepped from his gray SUV.

It was just past seven p.m., but it was already dark.

A bright porch light illuminated the stone pathway leading to Sarah Chamberlain's front door.

His boss had gotten Sarah's frantic call, and Ruger had been sent here to assess the situation and help the woman.

Help might mean whisking her away from here.

Or it could mean offering her a listening ear and reassurances.

The main thing he needed to figure out was whether or not the danger she felt was real or imagined. They had no reason to doubt her, but they had learned that many of the women they helped continued to live in fear.

There had been many instances where women in their program had thought the person they were running from had found them when, in fact, they had not.

As Ruger started toward the house, he passed the attached garage. Peering in the window, he saw a dark-colored sedan inside.

Good. Sarah should be home.

A few seconds later, he knocked at her door.

There was no answer.

Ruger peered in the window and spotted a purse on a table near the door.

Sarah was clearly home.

Was she not answering out of fear? Because she was in the shower?

She should know he was coming. His team had sent her a message last night.

She should be expecting him.

Tension snaked up his spine.

He left the porch and walked the perimeter of the house. No neighbors were out here to see him or to call the cops.

Privacy was both a blessing and a curse when in hiding.

As he walked, he peered in the other windows, most which were obscured by blinds or curtains.

But as he caught glimpses of the home's interior, he didn't see anyone inside. Didn't see any signs of a struggle.

So, where was Sarah Chamberlain?

He reached the deck and paused.

That's when he saw the silhouette of a woman in the lake, illuminated only by the moon. From the looks of it, she was walking out into the lake. Her body sank lower until only her head and shoulders were visible.

What was she doing? That water had to be in the fifties, and snow-capped mountains stood in the distance.

It wasn't safe to be in water that cold for long—and definitely not at night and while alone.

A sense of urgency filled Ruger.

He stripped off his jacket and left it with his bag on the deck. Then he sprinted toward her.

Was that Sarah? Had someone forced her out there?

Her ex-husband?

He didn't see anyone else around, but Ruger couldn't be sure.

He only knew he needed to get the woman out of the water before it was too late.

CHAPTER
TWO

SARAH COULDN'T BREATHE.

Her lungs felt ready to burst, as if someone had put a corset on her and pulled the strings tighter and tighter.

She couldn't reach the bottom of the lake anymore.

Her arms flailed in the water as she tried to remain afloat.

She glanced back at the shore, knowing she needed to head back.

But when she saw the tall, broad figure dashing toward her, second thoughts hit her.

Maybe her odds were better out here in the lake.

She looked back at the massive horizon of water in front of her. She knew the lake was more than a hundred feet deep in certain places.

She wouldn't last out here long.

But she wouldn't last at the hands of her ex-husband either.

She had an impossible choice to make.

Before she could decide, the sound of someone diving into the water filled the air, followed by arms slapping the surface.

The man—possibly Bryce—was coming for her.

As panic seized her, Sarah froze again.

Then she began to sink. Water covered her head until blackness surrounded her.

The cold was messing with her mind—and body. It was beginning to shut her down.

She couldn't think clearly.

Was it Bryce? Was he getting close? When he found her, would he hold her under the water? Make her pay for the humiliation she'd caused when she left?

She flailed again, desperate to get to the surface. To breathe. To see where he was now.

Bryce would make her death look like an accident, wouldn't he?

He would get away with murder.

No . . .

As soon as a hand gripped her wrist, survival instinct kicked in.

She flung her legs out, determined to fight for her life.

Bryce wouldn't destroy her again.

Ruger had no idea what was happening right now.

As far as he could tell, no one else was out on this lake with Sarah.

Had she been trying to kill herself? Was she naive enough to think she could take a swim this late at night? And alone, at that?

Right now, it didn't matter. All that mattered was saving this woman. Getting her out of the water and warm before hypothermia kicked in.

But as Ruger grabbed her arm, she thrashed.

Panicking in a situation like this could end up getting them both killed.

Thinking quickly, he dove underwater and circled her waist with his arms.

She continued to kick. To buckle.

Her elbow flew back and hit his ribs.

The woman had some fight left in her. He couldn't deny that.

He had to calm her down.

The two things he had on his side were his strength and his training.

He managed to pull the woman to the surface, where she sucked in a deep breath.

Then immediately, she began fighting against him again. Her fist flung into his jaw. She kicked his shin. Her entire body writhed with desperation.

One of Ruger's arms remained around her waist. The other treaded water and kept them afloat.

But she wasn't going to make this rescue easy.

"Relax," he murmured in her ear. "It's me."

She listened to his voice as if trying to place him.

Then without asking any questions, she burst to life. She elbowed him in the side again.

This time Ruger hadn't been expecting it.

His grip on her loosened.

As it did, she began to swim away—toward the middle of the lake where the deep water could swallow them both whole.

SARAH WASN'T sure where she was going. She only knew she had to get away from this man.

The voice didn't belong to Bryce.

This had to be someone he'd hired. A professional hitman.

It was the only thing that made sense.

Of course, Bryce wouldn't want her to die easily.

He wanted her to suffer.

That was just the way he did things.

Despite the numbness that captured her, Sarah managed to glide through the water away from that man.

Until fingers wrapped around her ankle.

More panic washed through her.

She continued stroking her arms through the

water, hoping the motion was stronger than the man's grip—even though she knew it wasn't.

The next instant, he tugged her toward him, and his arm went around her waist again.

He pulled her against his solid chest.

"Stop it!" he said. "I'm trying to help you."

Help her? Sarah doubted that.

"We're both going to drown if you don't listen to me," the man said. "We have to get out of the water. You need to get dry and warm. Now."

She wanted to ask him who he was. But as she opened her mouth, no words left. In fact, numbness spread through her entire body until moving even her mouth seemed impossible.

The realization caused another round of panic to rush through her.

She'd been out here long enough that it was no longer possible to fight.

The icy water had absorbed her energy, stealing it from her until she was helpless.

As blackness began to close in around her, Sarah shut her eyes.

She had no idea if she would wake up again.

Her last thought before drifting into nothingness was, *God, forgive me.*

Ruger had to get this woman back to the house.

They didn't have much time.

He'd spent entirely too much energy struggling with her.

Still treading water with his free arm, he glanced behind him.

The shore was probably twenty yards away now.

That was doable.

Sarah was no longer fighting him—a good and bad thing.

Good because she wouldn't slow him down.

Bad because she could be—and probably was—hypothermic.

Moving more quickly, he swam toward the shoreline.

As soon as his feet touched the bottom of the lake, he stood.

He lifted Sarah out of the water and into his arms.

Her body was limp in his grasp.

He prayed it wasn't too late.

Moving quickly but carefully, he maneuvered over the rocky shore then up the gravel path toward the deck.

He twisted the back door handle and shoved his shoulder into the door. It was unlocked.

Pushing it open the rest of the way, he hurried inside and found the bathroom.

Carefully, he set Sarah in the tub and turned on the water. He waited until the water was just warm enough to get her body temperature back up and then turned the shower on.

As the spray fell over her body, he patted her cheeks. "Sarah. Wake up."

But there was no response.

Ruger didn't think she had water in her lungs. She seemed to be breathing okay without a rattle in her chest. Thankfully, her pulse still felt strong.

He patted her cheeks again, but she only moaned.

He might need to call 911.

He wanted to handle this on his own if at all possible. It was better not to get anyone else involved. They would ask too many questions and might discover her true identity.

But he couldn't let her die either.

He checked her pulse.

Felt her heartbeat.

It was still strong.

Relief rushed through him.

At least, she was still alive.

Ruger let the warm water spray her another moment.

Then he ran through her house, trying to find blankets or anything else to keep her warm.

He'd never failed an assignment yet.

And he didn't want to start now.

CHAPTER
FOUR

SUDDENLY, the blackness in her mind disappeared.

Sarah sat up with a start and gasped in a desperate, almost wretched breath.

She was cold. So cold her bones hurt.

Looking up, she saw the spray of water cascading over her.

She was in her bathroom.

In the shower.

Alone.

She collapsed against her bathtub again.

What had just happened?

How had she gotten here?

As the questions fluttered through her mind, a shadow filled the doorway.

Alarm rushed through her.

But as she soaked in the man's features, she realized he wasn't Bryce.

This was the man who'd taken her from the lake.

He must have brought her here.

But could she trust him?

Sure, he'd rescued her. But that didn't mean he didn't have nefarious intentions. Trusting strangers wasn't an option right now.

Not if she wanted to live to see another day.

The dark-haired man stepped closer, hair still dripping. Clothes still drenched. His face, shadowed with a beard, somehow seemed trustworthy.

But that didn't mean he was.

Sarah tried to scoot away. But the tub surrounded her—trapped her.

There was nowhere to go.

"It's okay." His voice sounded low and serious as he stepped toward her. "I'm Ruger. I'm here to help you."

She pulled her arms across her chest, desperate for something to shield her from this guy.

He turned the water off and knelt beside her. "I brought you some clothes. You need to change so you can get warm. Your life depends on it. Do you understand?"

She stared at him a moment, waiting for his words to settle in her mind.

Finally, they did.

She nodded.

At least, if she was out of the bathtub and dressed maybe she'd have a fighting chance.

With more tenderness than she had anticipated, the man—Ruger—held her arm as he helped her from the tub then wrapped a towel around her.

It took a moment, but finally she found her balance as she stood on the cool tile floor.

With her wet hair dripping in her face, she stared at the man, knowing she must look feral.

Maybe that was a good thing.

Maybe that would keep him on edge.

Instead, he stared at her, his gaze still steady. "I left the clothes on the bathroom counter. I'll be in the hallway if you need any help. Understand?"

Sarah nodded.

She understood completely.

She understood that she needed to do everything in her power to get away from this guy. She knew how men operated. The kindness this man portrayed was just a mask. When that mask disappeared, it would be replaced with an image of who he really was—a monster.

Life experience had taught her that—in the most painful ways.

Ruger waited in the hallway and ran a hand over his face. He needed to change clothes as well, but right now his energy and attention had to be focused on Sarah.

He'd worry about himself later.

Because he wasn't convinced Sarah was going to let him help.

Why did she still seem so scared of him? It didn't make any sense. She knew he was coming.

But he'd cross that bridge later.

Keeping her alive was his first priority.

His phone was still outside where he'd left it on the deck when he'd taken his jacket off. He needed to call his boss, Charlie Soldier, and let her know what had happened.

But first he needed to be able to tell her that Sarah was okay.

He couldn't do that yet.

Finally, the bathroom door opened, steam escaping, the faint scent of flowers along with it.

He watched as Sarah stepped out, her features drawn.

Her dark hair hung wet and clung to her face. But at least she had on some warm black yoga pants and a sweatshirt now, along with some fuzzy blue socks.

That was a relief.

He swallowed hard, knowing he needed to move on to the next step of her recovery plan. "I'm going to start a fire now, and I want you to sit in front of it. With some blankets. It's either this or we go to the hospital."

His words seemed to shake her, and she pulled in a raspy breath. "No hospital."

"I understand. Do you need help getting to your living room?"

She stared at him another moment, something nearly unreadable in her gaze. Suspicion. Fear. Distrust. Uncertainty.

Finally, she shook her head. "No, I'll be fine."

Somehow, Ruger doubted that.

He took a step back and waited for her to lead the way. He wanted to walk behind her just in case she was unsteady.

But as she passed the kitchen counter, she lunged across it.

Her fingers closed over the handle of a butcher knife in a wooden block there.

Then she turned to him, the knife outstretched and fire flaring to life in her eyes.

Ruger's father had taught him an important lesson once when Ruger was twelve and out delivering newspapers. Ruger often came across dogs while enroute. His father had said: a scared dog is more dangerous than a mean one.

As he stared at Sarah, he couldn't help but think that was true of people also.

Sarah glared at him, a wild look in her gaze. "You need to leave. Right now."

CHAPTER
FIVE

SARAH HAD SEARCHED for something in the bathroom that might help her defend herself.

Shampoo and a hairbrush just wouldn't do.

But this knife she held would.

The man in front of her stared at her, his eyes wide.

Even though she wielded the knife, he remained calm and in control.

For some reason, that realization made her feel even more unnerved.

"You don't want to do this." Ruger held up a hand as if she were a tiger he needed to tame. "I'm here to help you."

"Who are you?" Sarah stared at him, not daring to show any more weakness. She'd already shown enough. Too much.

"Like I said, I'm Ruger. Ruger Stark. I'm from Vanishing Ranch. Charlie Soldier sent me."

Her muscles loosened but only slightly. "She didn't tell me she was sending someone."

"Yes, she did. I was there when she was talking to you on the phone yesterday. I heard your voice."

Sarah shook her head, wishing she could get rid of the cobwebs in her mind.

She couldn't think clearly.

Was something wrong with her?

This man sounded so convincing.

But Sarah couldn't remember that part of the conversation.

It didn't make any sense . . .

Was he trying to trick her?

Ruger held out a hand but didn't attempt to take the knife from her. "I promise you, Sarah, I'm here to help you. But I need you to trust me."

"I don't trust anyone." Her voice trembled as she stared at him, wishing his face didn't look so trustworthy.

"I know you've been through a lot." His voice still sounded even and calm.

It was almost as if he didn't understand that Sarah was holding a knife. As if this were a mundane, everyday situation.

"If I were in your shoes, I'd have trouble trusting

anyone also," he continued. "What can I do to prove that I won't hurt you?"

Something seemed to crack inside her. Not her stubbornness, however. Instead, it was a cacophony of fears and anxieties that had built up over the years.

"Nothing. There's nothing that you can do," Sarah finally said, her voice just above a whisper. "I won't—*I can't*—trust anyone again."

She couldn't even trust herself anymore.

A tear rolled down her cheek, and she silently cursed it.

"Sarah . . ." Ruger took a step closer. "Please. You need to put the knife down. I don't want to hurt you."

He sounded genuine.

But what if she put the knife down, only to discover this Ruger guy was just tricking her?

She wouldn't put it past Bryce to set up something like this.

He was that kind of person. The kind who liked making her feel stupid.

As she stared at the man in front of her, she realized she had a choice to make.

If she didn't choose wisely, she'd most likely die.

Ruger had no idea what Sarah would do. He saw the clashing emotions in her gaze.

So, he didn't make any moves.

Instead, he waited, ready to disarm her if necessary.

But time wasn't on her side.

Her teeth began chattering again. Her skin remained pale.

She wasn't out of the woods yet.

She needed warmth.

How could he make her see that?

"Sarah . . . you're cold. Let me help you."

She stared at him, lowering the knife only slightly.

"I'm not ready to die." Something raw sounded in her words.

"I have no intention of hurting you or letting anyone else hurt you. If you put the knife down, we can talk. You can get warm. I'll make you a hot drink. Coffee or cocoa? Whatever you want. Are you hungry?"

She shrugged as if she didn't know the answer.

Something about her was off, he realized. Ruger wasn't sure what, but it almost seemed like maybe she'd taken something.

He had looked at her files. She had no history of

drug abuse—prescription or otherwise. Maybe she'd hit her head. Had a panic attack.

He'd have to figure that out later.

She jabbed the knife toward him one more time, looking as if she was ready to make a move.

Before she could, her knees buckled, the knife fell from her hands, and she collapsed onto the floor.

CHAPTER
SIX

WHEN SARAH CAME TO AGAIN, she was lying covered in blankets on some pillows on the floor. The fire blazed beside her, warming her skin.

Everything rushed back to her, clearer this time than earlier.

She sat up and looked around until her gaze stopped on the man who'd rescued her.

Ruger.

He'd changed into dry jeans and a black T-shirt.

The man had a strong build, dark hair, a barely-there beard, and chocolate-colored eyes that reminded her of a Hershey's Kiss.

He didn't make a move as she stirred. Instead, he remained sitting on the couch behind her with his elbows perched on his legs as he watched.

"Do you feel better?" he finally asked.

She glanced around, checking to make sure there was nothing around her that should set off any alarms.

Everything appeared to be in place.

Her heart slowed.

"I could use some water," she finally said, realizing her throat was dry.

"I'll be right back." He walked into the kitchen.

A teapot was already heating on the stove, so he poured a cup of steaming water into a ceramic mug. As he started back toward her, he set the mug on the coffee table and paused beside her.

"You're going to need to sit up." He reached for her.

Sarah expected to flinch at his touch.

She didn't.

He gently braced his arm behind her and helped her into a sitting position. Then, remaining in his squatted position, he handed her the drink. "It's warm, but it shouldn't be so hot that it scalds you. Take a small sip first, just to be sure."

Sarah brought the mug to her lips and took a sip. It was just as he said—soothingly warm.

She held the mug, her fingers wrapped around it as she soaked in its warmth.

More of the fog cleared from her head.

Yet her thoughts still felt confusing and almost blurry.

What exactly had happened tonight?

She'd almost felt like another person had been living through her. Like she was there and aware of her actions but unable to control them.

The whole episode made no sense.

She glanced at Ruger, hoping that both gratitude and apology showed in her gaze. Gratitude for his rescue, apology because she'd threatened to kill him.

He must think she was off her rocker.

"In case you didn't pick up on this earlier—you were a little out of it—I'm Ruger, and I'm with Vanishing Ranch."

She nodded, hating how her head throbbed. "I talked to Charlie, but she was supposed to get back with me."

He twisted his head. "You remember talking to her?"

She squinted. "Why wouldn't I?"

He twisted his head even more, almost as if confused.

Sarah knew she was missing something, knew that her thoughts were fuzzy. Had they already had this conversation?

Finally, she said, "I'm sorry. I'm really not sure what's going on at all."

"I'm not either." His eyes narrowed, and he frowned. "Let's just work on getting you warm, and then we'll try to figure out what happened."

Ruger waited while Sarah drank her water.

Her hair had dried and fell into soft waves around her heart-shaped face

The woman was beautiful. Ruger had known that from the moment he'd seen her photo in the file.

But he hadn't expected her to act so neurotic. Her story didn't make sense, and he needed to discover why.

He was still trying to figure out what was going on. Had she had some type of mental break? Had the pressure of starting a new life gotten to her? Or were other factors involved right now? Substance abuse maybe?

Because if she'd seemed this unstable when she had been at Vanishing Ranch, Charlie would have made note of it.

Something was wrong.

After a few moments, Sarah put her mug down and tried to stand. Ruger rushed to help, wrapping an arm around her waist. He led her to the couch closest to the fire and waited until she lowered herself there.

Then he grabbed the blankets that had been around her and tucked them around her again. She still needed to stay warm.

"Do you need more water?" He stared at her, waiting for her answer.

She shook her head, almost appearing self-conscious as she pushed a strand of hair behind her ear. "No, I'm fine. Thank you."

Ruger sat beside her—careful to leave a good four feet between them—and turned to talk. "What happened tonight, Sarah?"

She rubbed her forehead and closed her eyes. "I'm not sure. I thought Bryce, my ex-husband, was coming. I knew I had to leave. To get away. Then I started walking. Next thing I knew, I was in the lake and the water was over my head. Then I saw you, and I thought Bryce had hired you. I panicked."

"I've read your file. I know you're not the irrational type. Fear can cause us to do things that aren't normal at times. There was more to it than that, wasn't there?"

She lowered her hand from her face and brought her arms across her chest as she stared at the fire. "I don't feel like myself, and I don't know why."

Ruger's thoughts raced through the possibilities. "Maybe I should get you to a doctor—"

"No!" Her voice sounded almost frantic. "I don't like doctors."

"But you're a nurse."

She took a deep breath as if trying to calm herself. "I work in home healthcare, so I don't have to interact with doctors all that much. That's the way I like it."

Ruger nodded slowly, understanding where she was coming from.

Her ex-husband was a doctor . . . and a vile, vile man.

Sarah's gaze met his again. "Did you come here to take me back to Vanishing Ranch?"

He swallowed hard before saying, "Not yet. First, I need to know if the threat is real or not."

Her eyes widened. "I'm telling you, something's off lately. I can feel it. You don't believe me?"

"I didn't say that. I just need more clarification. Sometimes when we're afraid, we see things that aren't there."

"But—"

Ruger raised a hand so he could finish. "Like I said, it's not that I doubt you. But Charlie spent thousands of dollars to create this new identity and life for you. There's no way that Bryce should've been able to find you. So, I want to stick around a couple of days to see for myself. At the first sign there's any danger, I'm taking you away from here and to safety. Understand?"

Sarah stared at him a moment as if she wasn't sure if she understood or not. Finally, she nodded. "But you can't be with me all the time. I have to go to work. I have responsibilities. I have bills to pay."

"I'm hoping you can tell people I'm a family friend who came to visit. That way it won't seem strange if I'm hanging around with you or maybe even driving you places."

She stared at him another moment before finally nodding slowly again. "I suppose that makes sense."

Ruger leaned closer, feeling even more determined than ever to protect Sarah—especially considering this was his first solo assignment. There wasn't room to fail—on multiple levels.

"We're going to figure this out, Sarah," he told her. "But you're going to have to be honest with me."

CHAPTER
SEVEN

SARAH KNEW why Ruger had said the words.

She was acting erratic.

Even she couldn't explain it.

Maybe the stress of everything was getting to her. She'd read case studies before about the impact of stress on the brain. Maybe that's why she wasn't acting like herself.

And she didn't sleep well last night.

But she hadn't slept well for months. Maybe even years.

Sarah rubbed her forehead again, finally feeling warm. Her shivers had stopped.

She hated that this was all happening.

Hated that this was what had become of her life.

She'd once had hopes and dreams. She'd thought that handsome, wealthy Bryce Daniels was the one she would make her future with so she could see those dreams come to fruition. For the first year of their marriage, that seemed like the case.

Then life had morphed into a nightmare.

Especially when Bryce tried to kill her and then made it sound like she was going crazy.

Everyone had believed him instead of her. After all, he was an esteemed doctor, the one whose family was established in the area and well-respected.

Sarah was just a small-town girl Bryce had fallen in love with.

Regret filled her. It did every time she thought about Bryce.

If only she'd recognized the signs before she married him.

But he'd hidden them too well. He'd been so charming.

"Maybe you should get some sleep tonight." Ruger straightened. "Then in the morning, we can talk and figure out a plan. You're supposed to work tomorrow, right?"

"Yes, I have eight patients to see."

"In the morning, we'll get our story straight. Together, we'll figure this out."

Ruger sounded so certain. She hoped he was correct.

But, deep inside, Sarah didn't think anyone

would ever be able to truly protect her from the monstrosity who was her ex-husband.

As soon as Sarah was in her bedroom, Ruger checked all the windows and doors.

The place was locked up, and the alarm was on.

As far as he could tell, everything here was safe and secure.

Just to be certain, he turned the lights out and glanced out the back window.

He scanned everything outside but saw nothing to cause concern.

Whatever was happening here, he didn't like it.

Right now, he needed to call Charlie. Even though it was late, he knew his boss would want to know what had happened.

Charlie ran Vanishing Ranch, and the woman was a true professional in every sense of the word. She was beautiful, business-smart, and tough. She'd made it her mission in life to protect people who had no resources at their disposal. Mostly, that was women in bad relationships. Occasionally, it was a man. But always it was someone desperate and in danger.

Someone had told Ruger a statistic about how

many people they'd helped since the ranch opened a few years ago. He'd forgotten exactly what the number was, but it was a lot.

These people paid nothing. Charlie footed the bill for everything.

She had money from when her father had been a pro-football player. But she was also savvy and had connections with people with money and power. They often donated to help the ranch stay afloat.

Relocating people and helping them start new lives wasn't cheap. But, as Charlie always said, it was worth it. Every life was worth it.

The guys who worked for her were referred to as her angels, which Ruger found amusing.

He'd only worked for her several weeks, so he was still learning things about the organization. But the more he learned, the more impressed he grew.

Still standing by the window, he dialed. Charlie answered on the first ring, sounding surprisingly awake and alert. Ruger gave her a quick rundown of this evening's events.

When he finished, she let out a grunt. "We had Sarah evaluated by a psychologist—just as we do everyone—and she seemed fine."

"Do you think the stress of the situation got to her?" Ruger kept his voice low just in case Sarah was still awake and listening.

Charlie let out a sigh. "I suppose it's a possibility. There's been no direct proof that anyone's been watching her. Just a feeling, she said. She did say once that some things in her cabinet had been rearranged. That could be true, or it could just be an oversight on her part."

"I wish I could take her to a doctor to be checked. But she's refusing." Ruger shifted as he stared outside, still on guard. "What do you want me to do?"

"I wish I had more guys to send you so you weren't there alone. But that's just not possible right now, not after we rescued that truckload of women coming in from Mexico."

Three days ago, his team had gotten word about a human trafficking operation. They'd managed to save the women—thirteen in all—and take them to the ranch.

They'd never taken in that many women at once, so it was all hands on deck.

But Sarah couldn't wait. That's why Charlie had sent Ruger here.

"I want you to keep an eye on things. Give her a few days. Then we'll check in and see how she's doing. At the first sign of danger, get her out of there. I've read about a lot of cases of abuse in these women, but hers was one of the worst."

Ruger's throat tightened at the words. He hated to hear that. Hated to know that any woman suffered at the hands of a man. It wasn't right.

Then again, after what happened with Khya, he had no room to talk.

Ruger had never hit her or hurt her in that way. He would never raise his hand to a woman. Ever.

It hadn't even been psychological abuse.

But she'd needed attention that he hadn't given her.

Ruger would bear the guilt of that for the rest of his life.

Her death was one of the reasons he came to work for Vanishing Ranch. He hoped to make amends for his mistakes.

He wasn't sure that would ever happen.

But he'd dedicate his future to trying if that's what he had to do.

Just as the thoughts went through his head, he saw a light flicker in the distance.

His breath caught as he watched.

As quickly as the beam had appeared, it was gone.

What was that?

Or an even better question—*who* was it?

That's what Ruger needed to find out.

CHAPTER
EIGHT

RUGER SLIPPED OUTSIDE, making sure that his gun was in his shoulder holster. He double-checked the doors and used his phone to make sure the alarm system was on.

If anyone tried to open the door or window while he was gone, he would know.

But right now, he needed to figure out what was happening out in these woods.

Needed to know if Sarah was truly in danger or not.

Ruger hadn't seen the light again—not after the first time.

But he remembered the direction it had come from.

He slipped in and out of the ponderosa pines,

juniper, and spruce, an evergreen scent surrounding him.

As he headed farther away from the house, a new sound filled the air.

Voices.

Ruger's muscles tensed.

But the sound wasn't hushed like that of people plotting something dangerous. It almost sounded . . . jubilant.

As Ruger crept closer, he saw another light. A different kind. Not a flashlight.

But a bonfire.

He paused behind a tree.

Four guys had set up camp out in the woods. A bonfire roared at the center of them, and they all roasted hotdogs, drank, and laughed.

Were they trespassing? He couldn't be sure. This might be just off of Sarah's property. A state park was located next to her.

He watched a moment, making sure they seemed okay.

But nothing about them seemed suspicious.

It appeared they were just four guys out for a weekend together. They were loud and they'd clearly been drinking, but otherwise they seemed unaware of Sarah.

Ruger felt a little better knowing that.

But now he needed to get back to her cabin . . . just in case."

Sarah awoke early the next morning, her head still throbbing.

Without looking for Ruger, she stepped into the shower. She wanted to avoid the man for as long as possible.

Last night's events . . . they were just embarrassing.

The whole experience wasn't like her.

Those events still didn't make any sense. She'd thought about it all night between fitful bursts of sleep.

By the time she stepped into the living room, she was already dressed in her pink scrubs.

Her eyes widened when she saw Ruger sitting on the couch with a cup of coffee. He was already dressed also, the makeshift bed he'd put together on the couch cleaned up. He looked bright-eyed and bushy-tailed, as the saying went.

"Good morning." He raised the mug in his hands. "I hope you don't mind, but I went ahead and made some coffee."

Actually, the fact that coffee was already made

was a wonderful blessing. It was the little things that sometimes meant the most.

"Thank you." She poured herself a cup.

Feeling slightly shy—or maybe it was apprehensive—Sarah paced over and sat on the couch across from him.

She turned toward him, not used to having anyone around in the morning. "Did you have a good night?"

The man didn't look any worse for the wear. In fact, Sarah had seen the circles under her own eyes in the bathroom mirror, but Ruger looked almost as if nothing had happened.

"I slept just fine. How are you feeling today?"

Sarah took a sip of her coffee before saying, "I feel okay. I just need some coffee and maybe some water."

He studied her for a moment, and Sarah looked down at her cup, not liking the scrutiny.

Yet, she couldn't blame him. He probably thought she needed to be in an institution.

"What time do you need to get going?" he asked.

Her gaze searched out the clock on the wall. "I have just a few minutes. I'd offer you something to eat for breakfast, but I usually just grab a granola bar on the go."

"You don't have to make any special accommodations for me. I'll be fine."

She stared at Ruger's face a moment. For some reason, he looked slightly familiar, but she didn't know why.

She somehow felt as if she'd seen him before.

Had he been in town watching her? Was that what she'd felt earlier in the week?

She couldn't be sure. But she wasn't going to ask right now either.

She knew he was just here to keep an eye on her. There was no need to strike up any personal conversation.

Sarah cleared her throat. "So, how does all this work? Are you going to follow me around or . . . ?"

"I'll drive you."

She started to say he didn't have to do that. That she could manage her day as usual. But the thought of not having to drive after last night was a relief.

Instead, she took a few more sips of coffee before setting down her cup. "I guess we should probably get going. My patients don't like to be kept waiting."

Ruger stood, his tall, broad frame filling the space. "Okay then. Let's go."

Part of Sarah felt better knowing that someone as strong and capable as Ruger would be with her.

Another part of her . . . somehow felt intimidated by his presence.

But beggars couldn't be choosers, as the saying went. And, right now, Sarah was a beggar at the mercy of others if she wanted to survive.

RUGER WAS glad Sarah hadn't insisted on driving. Though she seemed better today, he wasn't sure it would be safe to put her behind the wheel, considering her mental state.

As he drove them in his SUV, he observed the area.

The mountain town was beautiful with a cozy downtown, numerous parks, and sprawling evergreen trees. Glacier National Park wasn't far, so tourists frequented the area—as did hunters and fishermen.

From what Ruger had read, the country's wealthy had started moving to this area over the past couple of decades, buying up land and sending housing prices skyrocketing. He could see why people would flock to this scenic area.

"So how do you like it here?" he asked as his GPS rattled off directions.

"It's a great town. Everyone's friendly. Really, I have nothing to complain about . . . except the fact that I miss my family and friends."

Ruger frowned at her words. He could hardly imagine how hard it would be to give up everything in order to start over again. But, because of her circumstances, it was the only way to survive.

"I can imagine that would be difficult." He made a left turn down a residential street. "But you've had no contact with anyone back in St. Louis, right?"

"That's right. I've been tempted. I've even thought about hopping on a computer at the library to check out my family's social media posts. So, I can see my nieces and nephews and how much they've grown." She frowned. "But I haven't. Because I've been too afraid that might somehow trigger something."

"That's probably wise. Especially considering who you're dealing with." He glanced at her and saw her nod somberly.

A moment of silence passed.

"So, what exactly has happened that frightened you?" Ruger finally asked. "Charlie gave me a rundown on your history, but I'd like to hear about the most recent events from you myself."

Sarah glanced out the window, a forlorn expression still on her face. "I know it doesn't make sense, but I just have this gut feeling that Bryce is close, that someone is watching me. Then I came home the other day, and there was a new pair of fuzzy socks in my drawer."

"Fuzzy socks?"

"I know it sounds crazy, but I've always loved wearing them. Bryce hated them. I mean, really hated them. As soon as I moved here, I bought several pairs. Since I was no longer living under his dictatorship, I splurged."

"But you're certain there was a new pair in your drawer?"

She frowned. "Either that or I'm losing my mind."

"Anything else?"

"There was one other time . . . I thought for sure I could smell Bryce's cologne. I was so certain that I threw up. Then a moment later, the scent was gone, and I wondered if I'd imagined it all."

Ruger's jaw flexed as she told him the details. The pain this man had inflicted on her . . . it was unforgivable.

But was he the one behind this now?

"What's that look for?" Sarah asked.

"It's nothing."

"Clearly, you have something on your mind."

He let out a long breath and glanced at her as they came to a stop at a red light. "The truth is, I had my colleagues check on a few things. Your ex-husband has been at work all week. He's had appointments at the hospital, and he hasn't missed one."

Her face seemed to pale. "I don't know what to say then. Maybe I *am* losing my mind."

As Sarah checked on her patients, she couldn't stop thinking about Ruger's words.

Bryce had been at work all week.

Of *course*.

He wasn't here. He hadn't found her.

But what if he'd *hired* someone to find her? He had the means and could afford it. But did he have the connections?

If not, he could find the right people. She felt certain of that.

But if that was the case, how did she explain the scent of his minty cologne she'd smelled in her home?

She couldn't.

Unless she was losing her mind.

She frowned.

Maybe that really was the case. Maybe that was why she'd felt so out of sorts lately. She didn't want to admit it, but the possibility could be true. She'd been in the medical field for long enough to know that things happened sometimes—medical anomalies that changed a person. That changed how they acted. How they thought.

"The house is just up here to the right." Sarah pointed to a house on the corner.

Ruger followed her directions and pulled up to the house of her fourth patient of the day, a woman named Mary Snyder who had congestive heart failure. The seventy-something woman was a delight and awfully spry considering her health problems.

Just as before, Ruger waited in the car for Sarah as she climbed out. She skirted past the gold 1980s model Ford LTD and stepped up on the cheerful front porch. An intercom waited for her there as well as a security camera.

Apparently, Mary's son worked in the tech world and, even though he lived five hours away, he'd equipped his mother's house to have top-of-the-line security.

She rang the bell and waited.

Ruger coming with her seemed like a waste of his time, especially if all this trouble was just a figment of her imagination. But Sarah knew the man wouldn't leave, not if he'd been hired to protect her.

Bryce had always made her feel incompetent. He'd made comments about her capabilities. He'd even encouraged her to consider taking anxiety medication—acting as if he wasn't the one who caused her anxiety.

Those things messed with her mind after a while. Made her doubt herself. Made her feel unlovable, for that matter.

Her thoughts veered from Bryce when Mary answered.

The woman's face lit as she waved her hand, motioning for Sarah to come inside.

But as she did, Mary glanced beyond Sarah at the driveway, and her eyebrows shot up.

"New car?" she asked.

Sarah shook her head. "No, someone drove me today."

If possible, the woman's eyebrows shot up even higher. "A man?"

Sarah swallowed hard. "He's just a . . . a family friend."

"But he's not related?" Mary tilted her head as she studied Sarah without apology.

Sarah let out a little laugh. "No, he's not related."

Mary leaned forward to get a better view of Ruger. "He sure is handsome."

Sarah glanced back at Ruger as he sat in the car. He offered a nod and wave. He certainly had to be curious about what they were talking about.

"I suppose he's not bad-looking," Sarah finally said, although the words were almost begrudging. She didn't want to think of men in those terms.

No, it was better if she kept her distance. If she didn't allow herself to feel any attraction. If she didn't let herself even notice the men around her—no matter how handsome they might be.

"And you're so pretty," Mary continued. "I never could understand why you were still single. And I know a couple of guys have asked you out. That's what the ladies at church said."

Sarah felt more anxious than ever for Mary to get back inside her house and stop looking at Ruger. It didn't surprise her that some of the ladies at church had talked about her love life. But she'd always encouraged them not to.

"I'm not interested in love or dating," Sarah finally said. "I'm perfectly content by myself."

She wasn't sure if her words were totally true. They were *mostly* true, however. Sarah had been so burned by love that she never wanted to get herself entangled in a romantic relationship again.

But, every once in a while, when Sarah allowed herself, her thoughts drifted to a different place, a different life. One where she might have the chance of happiness again. One where Bryce hadn't single-handedly ruined her hopes for the future.

Then she'd come back to reality and remind herself not to let her mind go there. The only thing worse than broken dreams was having your hopes rise again only to crash. She just needed to accept that her fate was to be single and alone.

Then again, what kind of life was she living if she always had to be by herself? Maybe she would've been better off . . . better off if she'd . . . ?

Sarah wasn't even sure how to finish her thought.

Her throat tightened, and she snapped back to reality.

She ushered Mary back into the house and tried to change the subject, talking about the woman's low-sodium diet instead.

Just as she got Mary settled in her chair to take her blood pressure, Sarah's phone rang.

Because of her job, she had to answer.

She didn't recognize the number, though the area code was local.

She put the device to her ear and answered with, "This is Sarah."

But there was no response on the other end.

"Hello?"

Again, she waited.

But no one said anything.

Then she heard someone breathing heavily.

Her blood went cold.

Was this another sign, another subtle way of Bryce letting her know he knew where she was?

Or was she reading too much into this?

RUGER HAD TAKEN the opportunity while Sarah was inside to look deeper into her background.

Numerous news articles had popped up about Sarah—whose real name was Aimee Daniels—and her supposed death. There were many pictures of her and her then-husband, Dr. Bryce Daniels. They smiled in each of them.

But, beneath those smiles, something sinister had been going on.

Sarah had changed her look since then—of course.

In the photos, she was blonde with straight hair flowing well below her shoulders. Her makeup always looked perfect. Her clothing had been immaculate.

Now, she had dark-brown hair, with a touch of

wave, that was cut above her shoulders. She hardly wore any makeup. Her clothing of choice appeared to be either scrubs or loungewear.

To be honest, Ruger liked her new laid-back look much better. But she looked beautiful both ways. She was the type who could wear a trash bag and look gorgeous.

Sarah climbed into the SUV and slammed the door.

"Looks like you two were having an animated conversation there on the porch." Ruger nodded toward the wraparound porch surrounding the house.

Sarah's cheeks flushed as she fastened her seatbelt. "Mary thinks you're very handsome."

He let out a chuckle. "Well, I'm sorry she had to subject you to that topic of conversation."

"No, believe me—I'm sorry." When Sarah saw Ruger starting to put his SUV into Reverse, she knew she needed to stop him. "Wait. I got a call while I was meeting with her. No one said anything on the other line."

Ruger shifted the SUV back into Park, all his attention suddenly on her. "Wrong number?"

Sarah shrugged. "It sounded like someone breathing on the other end."

"Maybe it was a patient calling you who needed

help."

She pressed her lips together in a frown. "Maybe, but I didn't recognize the number. I always program the numbers of my patients into my phone so I can know who's calling. I suppose it could have been a patient's relative or friend. That happens. It *was* from this area code."

"I need you to send me that number. I'll check it out, just to be on the safe side."

"Of course." Sarah held up her phone. "What's your number? I'll text it."

He rattled it off, instructing her to add it to her contact list. Then she sent the text and leaned back in her seat.

Ruger's stomach let out a growl, and he glanced at the time. "For now, how about if we grab a bite to eat? Didn't you say your lunch break was next?"

"It is."

"Then you name the place, and I'll treat you to whatever you want."

"You don't have to do that, but we should go to Moose Head Junction. They've got the best burgers in town."

"As you wish."

Ruger followed her directions until they pulled up to an oversized log cabin situated off Main Street. A giant plastic moose head was displayed on the front, along with wooden letters proclaiming the restaurant's name.

As they walked inside, several people called hello to Sarah. She greeted them as well.

People in town seemed fond of her. That was a good thing—good that she'd found a place to belong. But Ruger realized it couldn't be as simple as it seemed, not considering the situation as a whole.

They found a booth in a corner, and Ruger sat with his back against the wall so he could observe everyone coming and going. As he situated himself, he remembered that phone call Sarah had gotten. It truly could have been an accident.

Or it could be a subtle threat.

That's what he needed to figure out.

A few minutes later, a friendly waitress took their order, and then he and Sarah were left alone. But that didn't last long. Another nurse, a local librarian, and someone from church stopped by to introduce themselves.

"The people here are definitely friendly," Ruger said once they were alone again. "This is a nice place."

"It really is. Wait until you taste the food." Sarah studied him for a moment. "So, where are you from, Ruger Stark?"

"Houston."

"And how long have you worked for Vanishing Ranch?"

"Only a couple of months."

Her eyes widened as if alarmed by his amateur status.

He shrugged, his gaze scanning the place before settling back on her. "If it makes you feel better, I worked for the Secret Service before I worked for Vanishing Ranch."

Her eyes widened even more. "The Secret Service?"

"That's right."

She nodded slowly, as if a thought brewed in her mind. Finally, she said, "That explains a lot."

Something about her words set him on edge.

Ruger braced himself for whatever she might say next.

"I knew I'd seen you somewhere before." Sarah narrowed her gaze as she studied Ruger. "I thought you looked familiar but, then again, I thought maybe I was losing my mind."

"You remember seeing me?" He tilted his head. "Where would that be?"

"On the news. You're the guy that saved the president's life several years ago." Her sentence ended with a touch of awe. "You're him, aren't you?"

Ruger nodded, not denying it. The same look of humility she'd come to expect remained in his gaze. "That was me."

"You did a whole slew of talk shows and interviews after that. You were hailed as a hero." More details flashed back in her mind. How long ago was that? Three years?

When Sarah had watched him on TV, she remembered thinking how handsome he was and that he seemed noble—almost in an old-fashioned way.

He'd saved the president, and now here he was protecting her.

It seemed surreal.

"That's correct." But Ruger's voice held no excitement or pride.

"And, if I remember right, you went on to be a commentator on several news outlets, didn't you?"

"I did for a while." He nodded stiffly.

She tilted her head, hating to ask so many questions. But she couldn't seem to stop herself. "And now you're here doing this?"

He shrugged, still nonchalant. "It's a long story."

Maybe it was. But now Sarah was more curious than ever about his history, his story.

Secret Service . . . Sarah mused as she stole a glance at Ruger.

She'd bet he had quite the stories to tell.

She couldn't remember all the details, but she thought something else had happened to him, something the news had reported before he disappeared as a commentator.

If she had some time, she might look into it to refresh her memory.

But for right now, their food was delivered—a bison burger topped with lettuce and tomato for Ruger and a grilled chicken salad for Sarah.

Ruger offered to pray, and they both lowered their heads. When he said amen, Sarah picked up her fork.

It was refreshing to eat with someone who wasn't ashamed to pray before a meal. Guys like that seemed to be becoming few and far between. Even back before she and Bryce were dating, it wasn't something she often experienced. But as someone who'd grown up in the church and considered herself a Christian, she certainly appreciated it.

Bryce had told her he was a believer. But his actions hadn't matched his words.

She'd found that out the hard way.

She glanced at Ruger and noticed his attention was drawn to a TV in the distance. A news story flashed across the screen about former President Bill Radar. The man was shown on the screen shaking hands with philanthropist Jack Earl.

Why was Ruger so interested in the news story? Was it because he'd saved President Radar? Did the two stay in touch?

As Ruger's phone buzzed, he glanced at the screen and frowned.

Immediately, Sarah's curiosity about his past disappeared. The urgency of her current situation overtook her thoughts again.

Did he have an update on the phone number? On something else pertaining to Bryce?

"Ruger?" She stared at him, waiting for an update.

His jaw twitched before he looked up at her. "I just got a report back on that phone number. Turns out it's a burner phone."

"A burner phone? Don't criminals use those?" Fear pulsed through her.

"I know it may seem like that in the movies. But people have legitimate reasons for using them—starting with saving money on their phone bill. It's nothing to get alarmed about . . ." He paused and rubbed his jaw. "Not yet at least."

CHAPTER
ELEVEN

RUGER AND SARAH went through the rest of the day with no problems.

He'd kept an eye out for anyone suspicious, but he'd seen nothing.

He tried not to make any judgments as to what was going on. Sarah's suspicions could be valid. He just needed more time to check things out.

After her last patient, Sarah climbed in the SUV and slammed the door. He couldn't read her expression.

Was she relieved? Anxious?

"Time to head back?" he asked.

She nodded and blinked several times as if struggling to keep her eyes open. "I suppose it's dinner time. But unfortunately, I don't have much at home to eat. I'm used to just having salad or soup."

"Don't go out of your way for me. I can stop and get my own groceries if that helps you out. You don't need to act as hostess."

She waved him off. "Don't be ridiculous. I'll share whatever I have. But I'm not much of a cook, let me warn you."

"If it makes you feel better, I didn't come here to try your cooking." He offered a quick—and hopefully reassuring—smile.

They headed back to her place.

As Ruger drove, he scanned the road, looking for a sign of anything suspicious.

But again, there was nothing. No cars followed them. No one watched from the street corner. Everything appeared normal.

Everything felt *safe*.

That should be what he wanted. But safe didn't match what Sarah said she'd experienced lately.

Finally, they pulled back up to Sarah's place. Ruger stepped inside her house first and checked everything out. He didn't see anything out of place.

However, as soon as Sarah stepped inside, she froze.

"What is it?" Ruger watched her expression, trying to figure out what was going through her head.

Only moving her eyes, she glanced around. "Don't you sense it? Something feels off."

Ruger glanced around, but he didn't get the same feeling she did. Then again, he didn't live here. He didn't know the place as well as she did.

"If someone had come in, the alarm would've gone off," he tried to reassure her.

"Unless somebody knows the alarm code."

Ruger pulled out his phone and checked the alarm history. But there were no new notifications since they'd left this morning. "None of the doors have been opened since we left."

He showed Sarah the screen, and she frowned.

She pulled her arms across her chest as if chilled and glanced around again, an almost listless look in her gaze.

"Then maybe I am just imagining all of this," she murmured. "But it certainly doesn't feel like it . . . not in my mind."

Ruger had insisted on making dinner, and Sarah didn't object.

He had thrown together some spaghetti with meat sauce, a salad, and garlic bread. Everything was surprisingly tasty.

It had been a long time since she'd shared a meal with anyone. Occasionally, someone from church had invited her over. She'd turned down any offers at first, but slowly she'd warmed up to the people here and had said yes more often.

A man named Pierce Denning had also asked her to dinner. Sarah had politely declined. Then he'd asked her out several more times. The man had been persistent, to say the least.

He lived three houses down on the country road where Sarah's house was located, and Sarah had taken care of his grandmother after she'd had a knee replacement.

Pierce was a podiatrist, who apparently was still paying off his loans from medical school as well as getting his own practice off the ground. Hence, he lived with his grandmother.

The man seemed nice enough, and he was certainly handsome and had a good job.

But Sarah's earlier statement was true. She had no desire to date anyone.

As Ruger cleaned up—he'd insisted—Sarah had taken a shower and gone through her nightly routine before wandering back into the living room. She normally watched TV to unwind in the evenings—if she wasn't sitting outside and watching the sunset, that was. But tonight, a light rain had started, and conditions weren't right to enjoy mother nature.

When she spotted Ruger on the couch, she observed him a moment. If he knew she was there, he didn't let on.

He was certainly handsome, with looks made for TV. That was probably why, after he'd saved the president, he'd become the face of the Secret Service. He was well-spoken, and he didn't come across as cocky, like some people in his position might.

But Sarah still had questions. Questions about how he'd gone from doing what he did to doing this.

Not that she was complaining.

She'd been cautious about him at first, but now that she'd gotten to know him a little better, she liked him. As a bodyguard, of course.

"Hey." He looked away from his laptop and over his shoulder at her. "Everything okay?"

She snapped from her thoughts and nodded. "Everything is fine."

"By the way, while I was waiting for dinner to cook, I installed more security cameras. This way we can monitor if anyone comes and goes." He nodded toward some devices above her exterior doors. "They're only by the doors—not in bedrooms or bathrooms or anywhere private."

She glanced at the small cameras. "You already had them on hand?"

"I keep some in the back of my SUV. We use them a lot when we're on assignment, and I like to be prepared."

"I guess so."

"Anyway, we don't usually install these on interior walls because we don't want to invade anyone's privacy. But in this case, we need to know if your intuition is correct."

Sarah stepped closer, a chill washing over her. "And what if it's not?"

Something unreadable flickered in his gaze. Was it compassion? Or did he feel sorry for her?

She wasn't sure.

"If that's the case, then we'll cross that bridge when we get there." His words remained slow and steady. "Right now, we just need to figure out what's going on in this house and if you're safe or not. That's our first priority."

She stared at him another moment before nodding. "Okay then. If it's all right with you I think I'm going to turn in for the night."

"That sounds good. We'll talk more in the morning."

With one last glance at him, Sarah disappeared back to her room.

Maybe tonight it would be better if she read a book instead of watching TV. Every time she looked at Ruger, she felt drawn to him. The feeling was foreign, something she hadn't experienced in a long time.

And she didn't like it.

Because men only caused one thing: pain. And she'd had enough of that to last a lifetime.

CHAPTER
TWELVE

SARAH SAT UP IN BED, a cold sweat across her brow.

She glanced around.

Everything seemed normal, but nothing felt right.

That familiar feeling of numbness spread through her.

Was she even awake? Or was this a dream?

She wasn't sure.

All she knew was that she was in danger.

Survival instinct filled her veins, and she threw her covers off.

She didn't bother to put any shoes on. Instead, wearing only her nightgown, she started toward the hallway.

She didn't know where she was going. She only knew her feet led the way.

Opening the back door, she stepped into the cool nighttime.

A soft beeping noise sounded, but she ignored it.

The air outside was chillier than it had been earlier, probably in the mid-forties. The light rain had turned into a fine mist.

Her gaze seemed pulled to the lake as if it were a magnet drawing her attention.

As if on autopilot, Sarah headed toward it.

She didn't know why, nor was there any urgency in her steps.

But she kept walking.

Everything would be better if she could just reach the lake.

No, Sarah. That's not true. You know it's not. Why are you heading this way?

The voice of truth whispered in the back of her mind. But it was hardly loud enough to make sense of it. Her impulses drowned out the voice of reason.

She kept walking until her feet hit the gravel path. She ignored the prick of the sharp rocks beneath her.

They didn't matter. *Pain* didn't matter.

Only the lake, which mesmerized her.

The water glowed like melted silver as pines stood guard around it, shrouding it with protection.

The water should be her grave.

Her watery grave.

It was what she deserved.

That's what Bryce had told her. That she was worthless. That if she died, no one would mourn her. That when God created her, it had been a life wasted.

She was halfway down the path when she paused.

Voices in the distance drifted to her ears.

Voices? Yes, there was more than one.

But who was out there?

Was someone on her property?

People didn't realize how sounds echoed across this lake. But sometimes that same fact made it difficult to discern how far away the noise was coming from.

Sarah glanced at the lake again, feeling as if she'd be betraying it if she walked away.

But her groggy brain had taken on a mind of its own.

She needed answers.

So, she turned to head toward the forest.

Once between the trees, broken branches on the ground dug into her feet. Limbs scraped her arms. Underbrush grabbed her ankles.

Darkness consumed the moonlight.

But she kept moving.

She had to find out where those voices were coming from.

Was it Bryce?

Maybe she should confront him head-on. Stop avoiding him. Stop living in fear.

As she passed a cluster of aspens, she heard a footstep behind her.

Was this it? The moment she would face her tormentor?

———

Ruger awoke with a start.

Something was wrong.

As his phone buzzed, he glanced at the screen.

The security system had been triggered. A camera showed movement outside the house.

He sprang out of bed, pulled on his clothes, and grabbed his gun. After slipping on his shoes, he hurried from the room. As he walked, he rewound the footage on his phone.

It was Sarah.

His lungs tightened at the sight of her walking outside in her white nightgown.

She'd left the house like that? It was cold outside. She wasn't even wearing shoes.

From what he was seeing, it appeared she was headed toward the lake.

But why would she do that?

And why did she appear to be in a trance-like state?

Something was going on here. He was sure of it.

Was she sleepwalking? Having some kind of nightmare?

Ruger had no idea. Whatever it was, he didn't like it.

He rushed outside and headed toward the lake.

But when he reached the shoreline, he didn't see Sarah.

Where would she have gone?

Had she decided to go for a late-night swim again?

The temperatures were even colder tonight than they'd been yesterday. A light mist fell from the sky, mixed with a few tiny snowflakes. Getting in the water was a bad, bad idea.

Ruger released a breath before pacing the shore.

But he still didn't see her.

What if she was already underwater? If that was the case, it would be nearly impossible to find her.

The lake was too large. Too deep. Plus, he wouldn't last long in those conditions.

Ruger's jaw tightened as he glanced around, adrenaline pulsing through him.

He had to figure out what to do.

And he had to figure it out now.

CHAPTER
THIRTEEN

SARAH FROZE and waited for another telltale sign of what was going on.

Had that noise come from Bryce?

Had he found her here?

She wasn't sure. It was hard to think straight. Her head spun. Her thoughts felt fuzzy and unclear.

"Can I help you?" a deep voice said behind her.

Slowly, she turned.

A man wearing jeans, a flannel shirt, and a puffy vest stood there, a flashlight in his hands. He redirected it from Sarah to himself.

He was probably in his early twenties, if she had to guess. She didn't get immediate danger vibes from him, but she didn't feel safe either.

She should've never followed the voices.

She should've gone to the lake instead.

She didn't say anything. She only stared at him and crossed her arms over her chest.

After a moment, the man stepped closer. "Can you talk?"

Before she could even answer—not that she was certain that she *would* answer—another man joined them. This guy was larger, more intimidating, and he stumbled a couple of times.

Had they been drinking?

Was that the scent she smelled?

"Who do we have here?" The big guy slurred his words.

"I don't know. I just found her walking in the woods."

"She almost looks like a ghost in that white night-gown," the big guy said.

He didn't sound as friendly. In fact, the more his words slurred, the more certain Sarah was he'd been drinking.

"Do you want to warm up by our campfire, pretty lady?" he asked.

This was a mistake.

Sarah took a step back. She needed to get to the lake.

"Billy . . ." the first man said, a wariness in his voice.

"What?" The word almost sounded defiant.

"She's the one who came to us. No one forced her here!"

Before Sarah could turn to leave, the big man took her arm and began leading her toward the bonfire in the distance.

She knew she should run. She should get out of here before things took a dark turn.

It was isolated in this area. These men had been drinking.

All in all, this was a bad combination.

Yet, as the man led her toward the campfire, she didn't pull away. Another part of her craved the warmth the fire would offer.

Maybe she'd get warm first. Then she'd seek solace in the lake.

She sat on a rustic, wooden bench, and glanced around the bonfire.

Four men were here all together—the one who'd found her, the big guy, and two others. One belched from the other side of the fire, and the fourth man laughed as if it were the most hysterical sound in the world.

The big man—Billy, according to the first guy—pulled Sarah closer until she was right up against him.

"I'd say the fun is just about to begin . . ."

Ice spread through her veins.

Suddenly, she knew the fire wouldn't help.

Her chill was born deep inside her.

Sarah pressed her eyes closed, wondering why she felt outside of herself and unable to control her thoughts and actions.

What was wrong with her?

Whatever it was, it very well could get her killed.

As Ruger stood on the shore of the lake, a sound echoed in the distance.

He glanced through the woods and thought he saw another light—one just like he'd seen the night before.

Were those campers still out there?

His shoulders tightened as possibilities—and worst-case scenarios—rushed through his head.

Sarah was out here. Alone. Wearing only a flimsy nightgown.

And likely not in her right mind.

He'd need to figure that last part out later.

Instead, he started through the woods, following the light. He moved quietly, quickly. There was no time to waste.

So many questions pounded through his head, questions he'd need to address at a different time.

But he didn't like the way this was playing out.

As soon as the group around the bonfire came into sight, he spotted Sarah.

A man had his arm around her shoulders and pulled her close. She tried to push him away, but his grip didn't loosen.

Based on the cooler and the empty beer cans lying around, these guys were seriously inebriated.

Ruger stepped into the light, his hands on his hips as he surveyed the situation. "What's going on here?"

One of the men—not the one beside Sarah but a smaller guy—rushed to his feet. "Nothing. We have a permit to camp here."

"I don't care about your permit." His gaze stopped on Sarah. "Sarah, come here."

She met his gaze, and her eyes widened.

She tried to stand, but the big guy beside her pulled her back down toward him.

"We didn't force her to be here," the man grumbled. "She wants to join us. Right, pretty girl?"

She glanced at the man with wide eyes before looking back at Ruger.

Fear and confusion marked her features.

"Take your hands off her." Ruger bristled.

"As soon as she asks me to, I'll let go." The big

guy sneered. "But, right now, she's operating on her own free will. Who are you? Her boyfriend?"

Ruger felt anger boiling inside him. "Don't make me tell you again."

The man's hand tightened around Sarah's waist.

But she appeared frozen with fear.

"Sarah . . ." Ruger repeated, desperate to get through to her.

She glanced up at him, her eyes nearly vacant.

"See? She doesn't want to leave," the big guy said.

Two of the other guys laughed. But the smaller guy said, "Billy, just let her go."

"Who asked you?" the man retorted.

Both of the men jumped to their feet, facing off with each other.

Ruger saw his opportunity. Although he wanted to teach Billy a lesson, he didn't want to draw any unnecessary attention to himself or the situation. It wouldn't be wise considering Sarah was in hiding.

Instead, he quickly reached over and grabbed her hand. He pulled her away from the bonfire and toward him.

It took a couple of seconds for Billy to notice.

When he did, anger burned in the man's eyes, the glow matching the campfire.

"What do you think you're doing?" The man

strode toward Ruger, his hands fisted and his words slurring.

"I wouldn't if I were you . . ." Ruger let the rest of his warning go unspoken.

This guy wasn't going to listen anyway.

He hadn't wanted it to come to this.

But this guy was going to regret ever putting his hands on Sarah.

SARAH CONTINUED TO BLINK. Continued to try to force her mind to return to normal.

But her thoughts spun out of control. So did her actions. So did . . . almost everything about her right now.

Her true self seemed to be a ghost lingering at the back of her subconscious, one she couldn't summon even as hard as she tried.

She watched as the man—Billy—lunged for Ruger.

She drew back and braced herself, unsure what was going to happen.

But in one swift move, Ruger had the guy by his shirt and pressed him up against a tree.

Immediately, the man lost some of his bravado. It melted like an ice cube in the desert sun.

"You obviously don't understand," Ruger growled. "I said leave her alone. Do you catch my drift?"

Billy stared at him a moment and seemed to sense something dangerous in Ruger's eyes.

This guy wasn't messing with an amateur. He was messing with a trained fighter.

A moment of admiration rushed through her.

Sarah held her breath as she waited to hear what the man would say, to see what would happen next.

Finally, Billy raised his hands in the air. "I got it, man. Sorry for the misunderstanding."

Ruger glared at him another moment as if testing him.

Then he released his grip—but not before turning Billy around and shoving him back toward his friends. "If I hear anything else from you guys, there *will* be consequences. Do I make myself clear?"

The guys muttered their understanding.

With one more scowl at Billy, Ruger placed his hand on Sarah's back.

His touch sent something through her.

An emotion she had no business feeling.

But she felt it anyway.

Ruger wasn't possessive. Of course, he wasn't. Because Sarah wasn't his. And they weren't romantically linked.

However, the protection he offered was something she hadn't even realized she longed for.

Yet, she did.

Ruger continued leading her away until the bonfire was barely a glow in the distance.

As she took another step and her foot came down on a sharp rock, she let out a whimper.

In one motion, Ruger lifted her into his arms.

He said nothing.

He didn't need to.

She'd walked straight into danger, yet there didn't appear to be judgment in his gaze.

He carried her the rest of the way to the house in silence.

And Sarah—despite her current mental state—knew that this man had just saved her from a terrible situation.

Ruger didn't set Sarah down until they were inside the house. He kicked the door closed with his foot and kept walking with her until they reached the couch.

Then he carefully lowered her onto the cushions and pulled a blanket over her to cover her thin nightgown.

She almost seemed childlike as she grasped the blanket to her chest and stared at him, her hair damp from the mist outside.

The steadiness present in her gaze earlier today was now completely gone. It was almost like she was a different person.

"Where's your first aid kit?" He stood, worry pulsing through him.

"Under the bathroom sink."

He grabbed it, came back, and knelt in front of her. Pulling out some gauze and ointment, he began to assess the scrapes on her legs and feet.

Sarah simply watched, not saying a word.

There was so much Ruger wanted to ask.

First, he'd get her wounds clean.

He pressed the last Band-Aid on her leg and then rose, tucking the remaining supplies back into the first aid kit and setting it on the coffee table.

"Let me get you some water," Ruger said.

He appeared a moment later with a warm mug of water and watched as Sarah took several sips. Then he sat on the edge of the couch and studied her.

"What happened tonight?" His voice was still calm and even, but there was a new sternness to it.

She shook her head, tears pressing at her eyes. "I don't know."

"Do you have a history of sleepwalking?"

"No, I don't."

"Have you had episodes like this before? Recently?"

She shivered. "The night before you arrived, I felt out of sorts. When I woke up . . . I had some dirt on my feet. I thought it was weird but . . . I didn't know . . . Then, of course, last night . . . I'm still not sure what happened. I don't know what's happening to me." She lowered her water and rubbed the side of her face as if a headache was coming on. "I know as a nurse that sometimes trauma can cause psychotic breaks and . . ."

"We don't know that's what this is. But I *am* concerned."

As Ruger stared at her sitting on the couch, he wanted to pull her into his arms. She looked like she needed someone in her corner—someone who wasn't a paid bodyguard but a friend.

How long had it been since she had any human touch? She was so isolated out here.

"Ruger . . . I'm scared of what I might do next," she whispered, fear saturating her gaze.

He wasn't sure how it happened—or even if it *should* happen—but as she leaned toward him, he wrapped an arm around her shoulders. She nestled her head in the crook of his neck, and Ruger held her.

There was nothing romantic about the embrace.

Even if Ruger wanted to strike up a relationship—which he didn't—that went against the contract he'd signed when he'd begun working at Vanishing Ranch.

He couldn't get involved with clients.

But he didn't consider this getting involved.

He just considered this being a decent human being.

CHAPTER
FIFTEEN

SARAH TRIED NOT to feel self-conscious the next morning as Ruger drove her to her first patient's house.

She didn't remember the last time she'd felt as vulnerable as she did last night. She'd been outside in her nightgown, for crying out loud! And she'd wept. Had shown weakness in front of a man.

Those were things she'd vowed to never do again.

Yet here she was, unable to hide just how vulnerable she truly was.

For some reason, she instinctively felt safe around Ruger. She knew he wouldn't try anything, that when he held her it was just a friendly gesture.

Sarah didn't understand what was happening to her.

She almost wanted to talk to Sheila, the head

nurse of the home healthcare organization she worked for. Sarah almost wanted to ask the woman to evaluate her, to see if something was wrong with her.

Maybe she had a brain tumor. That could account for sudden personality changes.

Sarah rubbed her arms, not liking the thoughts of that either.

But she simply didn't know what was going on.

Ruger didn't seem to think less of her. At least, if he did, he didn't act like it.

Just like yesterday morning, by the time Sarah had awakened, Ruger was already dressed, his bed cleaned up, and he sipped coffee on the couch.

He hadn't said much, just asked her how she'd slept.

But she'd seen him looking at his phone.

The security footage was on it.

The video showing her walking toward the lake.

She assumed if he had any ideas of what was happening, he'd mention it to her.

But, right now, he simply drove, his watchful gaze on everything around them as he did.

He pulled into the driveway and then turned to her. "You going to be okay?"

Sarah pushed a stray hair behind her ear. "Yes.

Thank you. Working feels normal. It helps keep me grounded."

She climbed from the car but paused. It felt strange not to say anything about last night. To ignore what happened.

Before shutting the door, Sarah leaned back inside. "Listen . . . I'm sorry about . . . everything."

Ruger's gaze locked with hers, and his voice sounded steady as he said, "It's okay, Sarah."

Something about the way he said those words made Sarah believe they were the truth.

Ruger watched as Sarah disappeared into the house.

She seemed to sense the need to apologize for things she wasn't responsible for. He supposed that was normal considering her past circumstances.

This morning, as he'd been getting ready, he found her well-worn Bible on the end table. Part of him was surprised because the Bible had what appeared to be years of notes and highlights inside. But the name on the inside cover was Sarah Chamberlain.

She'd only had that Bible for two years max, yet it got plenty of use.

His grandma used to say that a Bible that was

falling apart belonged to someone who wasn't. It was inspiring for him to see that Sarah was trying to rely on God through these circumstances.

He stared at the house Sarah had gone into.

Her patient was someone Sarah had been seeing for the past three months without any trouble. He knew that patient confidentiality was a serious thing, and he didn't want to impose on that. But he *did* want to know about any new patients she might be assigned. Just in case.

This morning, Sarah seemed like a different person. He couldn't get over the change from last night. When he'd found her in the woods, she'd seemed sullen and confused, as if she'd mentally checked out.

But this morning . . . Sarah seemed clear-headed and perky. That same nurturing look was present in her gaze, and her appearance was neat and respectable.

The shift was almost jarring.

Before too much time passed, Ruger grabbed his phone to check in with Charlie. She wanted regular updates on the situation. She answered on the first ring as usual, and Ruger told her about last night.

She clicked her tongue before letting out a *hmm* and saying, "How strange . . ."

"You're telling me." Ruger leaned his head back, stretching his neck. "I have no idea what's going on."

"Let me ask you this. Have you seen anything yet to indicate the danger around Sarah is real?"

"She got a phone call yesterday, and no one was on the other line. She seems to sense someone's been in her house, but there's no proof." He paused, hating to say this next part. "Right now, it almost seems like her biggest danger is whatever is going on inside her head."

Guilt flooded him at the words. But they were true. And he couldn't keep the truth from Charlie. She needed to know.

"She refuses to go to the hospital?" Charlie asked, something tapping in the background—probably her pen against her desk. She had a habit of doing that.

"She's terrified to go, mostly because of her ex-husband. I don't know what to do."

"We've never been in a situation exactly like this before." Charlie let out another breath. "There have been a couple of women we've relocated after their abusers found them. But it's been nothing like this. I just need you to keep an eye on things until we have some concrete proof about what's going on."

"I can do that." He paused, another question on his mind. "However, I know you hired me to investigate what happened to your father. This was supposed to be a pretty quick assignment, but it may turn out to take longer."

Charlie's dad, Benjamin Soldier, had left a prestigious career in football to join the military, but he'd been killed on the battlefield. Charlie believed there was more to his death than the government let on. Since Ruger had government connections, he'd been brought in to help find answers.

But he hadn't really had a chance to start looking much yet.

"I do want your help with figuring out what happened to my father," Charlie said. "But, right now, protecting Sarah is more important. Don't worry, I definitely plan on utilizing your knowledge of the Secret Service—and your connections."

"Of course. I understand." He paused. "But there is one other thing I think you should know. The TV was playing while I was having lunch yesterday, and I saw a news story about President Radar. It was about a charity event he was attending, and the footage showed him with Jack Earl, the president of NorthStar Media." NorthStar was a social media company that had recently taken the nation by storm.

"I know who he is."

"When I saw them together, it reminded me of something from my time in the Secret Service," Ruger continued. "You may or may not know that Jack has quite the reputation. He's single, and he likes to date around. In fact, he thinks he's God's gift to women."

Charlie snorted. "I've met that type before."

"He and the president met on several occasions. Of course, this is all supposed to be hush-hush. Anyway, the two of them also had a meeting with Alex Windsor."

"Who?"

"Alex was a government contractor who died two years ago in a car accident. But there were rumors circulating around the White House that he may have been involved with the terrorists who bombed that building in Florida."

"And you're saying the president and Jack met with this guy?"

Ruger clenched his jaw before saying, "That's right."

"Isn't that interesting . . ."

"I'm not saying the president was involved with that bombing. But it is a connection."

"Thanks for sharing. I'll look into it."

Ruger ended the call and glanced around again, always on guard. Always watching for potential danger.

That's what he'd been trained to do with the

Secret Service. If he had his way, he would be right beside Sarah right now.

But he didn't want to go overboard, not until he knew something for sure.

He only hoped that by the time he knew something for sure, it wasn't too late.

Like it had been with Khya.

THE REST of the day went without a hitch.

Sarah had packed a lunch to bring with her today because she knew her schedule was full. Ruger also had one, and they ate in between seeing her patients.

Just like yesterday, Ruger had been a good sport throughout the day. He didn't say much or offer any judgments. He simply drove her around, kept an eye open for trouble, and remained patient.

Sarah had to admit she was partially relieved when her shift was over. Relieved because she was ready to get home. She was tired from not getting much sleep last night and from the emotional turmoil.

But she also dreaded what tonight might bring.

In fact, she'd considered not falling asleep. Maybe

if she stayed awake, she could remain lucid. Maybe it was sleep that made her act crazy.

Back at the house, Ruger went inside to check things out first.

Thankfully, everything was clear.

They'd quickly stopped at the store to buy a few things for dinner. It was the same small grocery store they'd passed on the way to her house, one where things were slightly overpriced but convenient.

It seemed weird to be worrying about what to eat now that she had a security detail with her. Normally, she just ate whatever she could scrounge up. But having Ruger in the house somehow felt different.

Sarah actually liked it. She liked having a reason to think about menus. And a reason to keep the place straight. And maybe even a reason to look a little nicer than usual.

She hadn't been motivated to do any of that for the past year.

Besides, Bryce had always insisted she look a certain way. Keep the house a certain way. Cook certain meals.

Maybe that's why when she did finally escape, she'd abandoned all that.

It was totally different to do those things because

you wanted to rather than to do them because someone else expected—or demanded it—of you.

Sarah hadn't even known the extent of the stress it caused until she didn't have that pressure on her anymore.

Ruger set the paper bags of groceries on the kitchen counter and turned to her. "How about if I get a meal started while you get changed? Fajitas sound good?"

Gratitude filled her. "That sounds amazing."

Just as she thanked him and took a step toward her bedroom, someone knocked at the door.

Suddenly, all the relaxation Sarah had felt just moments earlier disappeared.

Ruger instantly went on guard.

Who was here?

He glanced at Sarah, who'd gone pale. "Are you expecting anyone?"

She shook her head, but he already saw her withdrawing, saw the fear setting in and threatening to control her.

He grabbed his phone and hit the camera button there.

A man stood on the doorstep—someone Ruger didn't recognize.

As the knock sounded again, Ruger showed Sarah the image. "Recognize him?"

Her shoulders seemed to relax, even though she offered a half eye roll. What was that about?

"That's my neighbor, Pierce," she said. "He actually lives with his grandmother three houses down. He's stopped by a few times before."

Ruger's gaze darkened. "Do you want to answer, or do you want to ignore him?"

Sarah seemed to consider his question a moment before nodding. "I'll answer. He knows I'm home, and I don't want him to overreact."

Ruger nodded. "I'll stay close, just in case."

She rolled her shoulders back before starting to the door and pulling it open.

A man in his early thirties with short blond hair and a lean build stood there. He wore a sweatshirt, joggers, and running shoes—expensive joggers and expensive running shoes. Ruger recognized the brands, which were prominently displayed on the clothing.

Sarah seemed to force a tight smile. "Pierce, I wasn't expecting to see you."

"I just thought I'd stop by to check on you," he said. "How's it going—"

Midway through the sentence, he paused and glanced beyond Sarah at Ruger. "I'm sorry. I didn't realize you had company."

Sarah stepped back, waving a hand through the air. "Oh, yes. I . . . um, this is . . ."

Ruger stepped in, trying to ease the situation. "I'm Ruger, a family friend."

Pierce stared at him, the man clearly trying to size him up. "A family friend, huh? Where are you from?"

"Houston," Ruger answered. "That's my SUV out there. With the Texas license plate." He called the guy out. Pierce had to know she wasn't alone. So why was he pretending to be surprised?

"Are you here visiting a while?"

"I'm not sure yet." Ruger tried to loosen his shoulders, but this man was putting him on edge. "That has yet to be determined."

Pierce seemed to stiffen as the conversation went on, almost acting cagey.

He turned back to Sarah. "Can I have a moment of your time? Alone?"

Ruger instantly tensed.

Alone?

That was a terrible idea.

The last thing Ruger needed to do right now was to make a scene.

But there was no way Sarah was stepping outside alone with this man.

SARAH OPENED HER MOUTH, struggling to answer.

Before she could come up with a good excuse as to why she couldn't talk to Pierce one-on-one, Ruger stepped in.

"Why don't you come inside instead?" he said. "I'm just starting to cook some dinner so that would be a great opportunity for you two to talk."

Pierce frowned as if he didn't like that idea. But, certainly, the man also had to know that refusing would only make him look suspicious.

A moment later, he stepped inside. "I can only stay a minute."

That was perfect. Sarah didn't say that aloud, of course.

But thank goodness for Ruger's quick thinking.

She crossed her arms over her chest as she turned to Pierce. "What's going on?"

He paused in the entryway and leaned against the wall. "I just wanted to check on you. I heard there have been a lot of unruly campers out at the state park. Some of them were arrested last night, apparently."

Her eyebrows shot up. Were those the same men she'd encountered?

Ruger said he didn't call the police on them, that it was better if the cops didn't get involved because they might ask him questions. She agreed with his assessment.

"I don't like the sound of that." Sarah studied Pierce's face. "You haven't had any problems, have you?"

"No, no problems at my grandma's place. But you're closer to the state park since your property backs right up to it."

"That's true. Thankfully, it's been pretty quiet out here. I don't usually see anyone from the park here on my property." She paused, questions circling in her head. Pierce lived close. Had he seen anything? Bryce? "You don't either, do you? Not that you probably come out this way that often."

Pierce let out what sounded like a nervous laugh

and took a step back. "No, I don't. Even though I *should* head to the state park more than I do."

Something about the way he said that made her wonder if he *did* come past here.

Not because of the state park.

But to check on her.

Maybe that was sweet. Maybe she should be grateful. If someone besides Pierce had done it, she might be.

But she sensed an insincerity about Pierce.

She'd learned to identify pretense after being married to Bryce for six years.

Pierce wasn't a safe person. He may not be the type to hurt her physically, but he simply wasn't someone Sarah wanted to be around.

Behind her, Ruger finished slicing some peppers and onions and added them to a pan. But she knew he had one eye and ear on this conversation.

Pierce stood there another moment, almost seeming awkward. Finally, he glanced at Ruger again and took a step back—almost reluctantly. "I guess I should go."

Relief washed through her. "Of course. Give your grandmother my regards."

His gaze lingered on Ruger another moment before he headed toward the door.

Ruger walked him out, said goodbye, and then locked the door behind him.

Only then did Sarah let her shoulders relax.

As Ruger cooked, he stole a glance at Sarah, uncertain if he should voice his thoughts. Yet he knew it was rarely healthy to keep secrets. Being open was usually better in the long run.

"That guy gives me bad vibes." He shrugged, lifting the spatula in his hands as the peppers and onions began to sizzle, adding their savory aroma to the air.

"Me too."

He studied her face. "Have you ever been romantically linked with him?"

Sarah quickly shook her head. "No, absolutely not. He's asked me out a few times, but I've always turned him down. I have no desire to date. But if I ever do get that desire again, Pierce will not be the man I go out with."

Ruger continued to observe her for a moment, trying to get into her head. "Why not?"

He checked the peppers and onions again.

Sarah moved to the breakfast bar and leaned against it, watching as he cooked.

She paused to think about his question. "Honestly? I know his type. He's the same as Bryce. He's a guy who likes collecting trophies. He wants a nice car. Designer clothes. A big house. A beautiful woman to accompany him."

"A lot of guys like a beautiful woman at their side."

She shrugged, almost looking forlorn. "I don't know how to say this without sounding stuck-up, and that's not the way I mean this. But for my entire life, I've never known whether a guy likes me for who I really am or for how I look. There are some men who don't care at all about who I really am, how I think, or how I feel. All they want is an armpiece."

Ruger heard the sincerity in her voice and knew she wasn't trying to sound stuck-up, as she had said. She really was remarkably beautiful, and many women like her might flaunt it and use their beauty to their advantage. But not Sarah.

"I'm sure that can be challenging." He added chicken strips to the pan. *I'm sure that can be challenging?* He couldn't have come up with something better than that?

He stirred the chicken, mixing it with the peppers and onions.

"Bryce really tricked me. When I first met him, I thought he was the type I just described. But he wined and dined me, as they say. When I talked, he listened to me. He made me think I was the only woman in the world." She rubbed her arms as if chilled. "But it was all a façade, and I fell for it. To be honest, to this day I sometimes don't trust my instincts because of it."

"I'm sorry to hear that. But you can learn to trust your instincts again. Not every man is like Bryce or Pierce."

"I know. But that type seems to be drawn to me." She frowned, but not in a pouty way. More like she was truly distressed at the thought—at the thought of no one ever loving her for who she was, only what she could do for them.

He turned off the burner as the chicken, peppers and onions finished cooking.

Then he glanced at her, one more thing on his mind.

"Sarah, have you ever considered that maybe it's not Bryce behind all of this? What if it's . . . Pierce?"

AS SARAH SAT down to eat dinner, she couldn't get Ruger's words out of her head.

What if this wasn't Bryce at all? What if it was Pierce?

Why did she seem to attract men like them?

The realization made her feel as if something was inherently broken about her. Maybe it was. Maybe *she* was the problem.

She picked at her food, her appetite waning.

"You don't like fajitas?" Ruger stared at her.

She shook her head. "I'm sorry, it's not that. I just seem to have lost my appetite."

He lowered his fork back to the table. "I know this has been a lot. But I also know that we don't have any time to waste, which is why I shared the theory about Pierce. Do you still really feel Bryce is behind everything?"

Sarah thought about it a moment. She *had* been totally convinced. But what if she was wrong? Who else would have known about the fuzzy socks?

She let out a long breath. "This seems to have his fingerprints all over it."

"I did follow up again today, and he's still at work. I know you believe maybe he paid someone to come here and do these things."

She nodded, nausea churning inside her. "I definitely think that's a possibility."

"We have a guy who's able to get into places on computers that most people can't. It's not always legal, but we're careful. Anyway, he looked into Bryce's financials today."

Her lungs seemed to freeze with anticipation. "And?"

Ruger shrugged. "There was nothing unusual. No big chunks of money that were taken out—money that would be needed to pay for . . . well, a hitman."

"How about cash withdrawals? Bryce is smart. He wouldn't—"

"There were no cash withdrawals either." Ruger's words almost sounded apologetic.

Sarah felt herself deflating. "There must be other ways Bryce could pay someone. There have to be."

"I'm not saying there aren't. I'm just saying we need to be openminded."

Sarah slipped her hair behind her ear as her gaze stopped on Ruger. "I understand."

"Is there anyone else besides Bryce and Pierce who might want to mess with your head? Who might have seemed a little too attentive? Certainly, you've had your fair share of guys who are interested in someone as beautiful as you are."

His words caused her breath to catch.

Did he think she was beautiful? That could be a blessing or a curse.

Or . . . it could just be that he'd said it matter-of-factly.

That was probably it. Ruger seemed like an upfront kind of guy.

And she greatly appreciated that.

"I'd definitely say Pierce is the main guy," she finally said.

"I'll look into him out of an abundance of caution."

Sarah rubbed her neck before admitting, "I'm nervous about tonight. About what I might do."

He leaned closer, his gaze softening. "How about this then? I'll keep an eye on you and stop you from doing anything before you ever leave."

Sarah swallowed hard. She wasn't sure how Ruger planned on doing that. But right now, she wasn't in a position to argue either.

After Ruger had cleaned up from dinner and while Sarah went to take a shower, Ruger planned to look into Pierce Denning.

But when a piece of silverware had fallen between the counter and the refrigerator, he'd found something as he retrieved it.

A receipt.

It was from the general store and dated last week.

And the item that was purchased . . . socks.

Could it be for the ones Sarah said had appeared in her drawer?

He frowned as he studied the receipt. It appeared whoever had made the purchase paid with cash.

Had Sarah bought them? Had she forgotten? Was she lying?

He didn't like any of the possibilities.

When the time was right, he'd ask her.

For now, he placed the receipt in his pocket and then sat down with his laptop to look up information on Pierce.

The man was originally from Minneapolis, though he had family roots in this area. He'd gone to medical school—but not the same one as Bryce. Ruger had checked.

Pierce appeared to be single, without children,

and he'd opened his own practice here in town a year ago. Ruger didn't see a criminal record or anything else that raised any red flags about the man.

Did that mean he was innocent?

Not necessarily.

Ruger would definitely be keeping an eye on him.

By the time Sarah emerged from the bathroom, it was already nearing eight o'clock. It would be a long night, and Ruger knew he needed some sleep. He wouldn't be able to operate at his best if he didn't get any rest.

But he also somehow needed to monitor Sarah.

For now, maybe they could get settled and talk a little more.

Ruger started a fire, and the flames crackled in the fireplace, adding just the right amount of warmth to the room. Sarah sat on the couch with a blanket thrown over her legs. Ruger decided to change into some joggers and a T-shirt, making sure to grab the receipt from his pocket.

He sank into the couch, wishing he didn't have to bring this up. But he couldn't avoid it.

"Sarah, about those socks you found . . ."

She tilted her head. "What about them?"

He pulled out a receipt. "I found this in the kitchen."

She took it from him and read the words there,

her eyes widening the more she stared at it. "So, you think I bought the socks?"

Ruger shrugged. "I don't know what to think. That receipt makes it seem like it."

She shook her head. "I didn't buy them."

"Then how did the receipt get there?"

"I have no idea. Maybe Bryce left it."

He opened his mouth to say more but then shut it again. He didn't have any answers.

"You think I'm going crazy . . . or lying," Sarah finally said.

"I didn't say that. I just want answers—like you do. I'm trying to figure this out. As soon as I have the chance, I'll visit the general store and see if any of the clerks remember anything. We'll get to the bottom of this."

"Thank you for not assuming the worst."

A few moments of silence passed, and Ruger gave her time to process the update.

Then he felt her gaze on him.

As he glanced at her, he saw the questions in her eyes.

He waited for her to say whatever was on her mind.

She did a few minutes later.

"If you don't mind me asking, have you ever been married?"

The question startled him. He hadn't expected it, and he wasn't sure he was prepared to answer.

"I was. For nine years. But she passed."

Her gaze softened. "I'm so sorry to hear that. Do you mind me asking what happened?"

His throat tightened as he forced back the memories that came with his answer. "Suicide."

It took all his energy to say that word. He didn't want to go into any more detail. Not now. Maybe not ever.

"I'm sorry." Regret filled her gaze.

"Thank you. But it's not something I like to talk about."

"Understood." She glanced at her hands as if she felt ashamed for asking.

Ruger wanted to reach out to her. To tell her that it was okay to ask questions. That it was okay to not see eye to eye.

He had a feeling that Bryce set her straight whenever she "got out of line."

Ruger wanted to reassure her.

But before he could, he noticed her eyes start to glaze.

His shoulders tightened.

She stared at the fire as if seeing right through the flames.

This was happening again, wasn't it?

What was it about the nighttime hours that seemed to bring out this side of her?

Ruger wasn't sure, but he braced himself for whatever this evening might bring.

CHAPTER
NINETEEN

"SARAH?"

She pulled her gaze up to meet Ruger's.

But her brain . . . it didn't feel right again.

Tears pressed at her eyes at the thought. If things remain on course as they had the past couple of nights, she'd only be aware she was losing control of herself at the very beginning of her episode. In ten or fifteen minutes, she'd feel as if she were outside of herself again.

"It's happening again."

Part of her wanted to ask Ruger if he'd handcuff her to a chair. To do *something* to ensure she didn't do anything stupid.

But she knew he was looking out for her. He would do whatever needed to keep her safe.

That thought should comfort her, but for some reason it didn't.

She felt too out of control already.

As the conflicting thoughts swirled in her head, her phone rang.

Her breath caught when she glanced at the screen and saw another unknown number.

Was this about a patient?

She glanced at Ruger. "Should I answer?"

He moved closer and nodded, but she sensed his apprehension. "Put it on speaker, please."

She did as he asked, mumbling a feeble, "Hello."

But, just as last time, there was no answer.

Only heavy breathing.

At once, she remembered being married to Bryce. Remembered him sleeping beside her. Remembered the sound of him breathing in her ear.

The phone clattered from her hand as bad memories began to strangle her. Ruger grabbed the phone and hit End before kneeling beside her.

"Sarah?" His voice sounded soothing, but it made no difference.

She was out of the driver's seat again.

"Sarah?" Ruger repeated.

She glanced around, suddenly feeling like the walls were closing in.

Bryce was here, wasn't he? Was he in her house? Was he watching her right now?

Sarah didn't know.

All she knew was that she had to run.

———

Ruger sensed the situation escalating. He lifted a prayer for wisdom on how to handle this.

He'd been trained for protection detail. But he'd never been instructed on how to handle a situation quite like this before.

"I need to go." Urgency strained Sarah's voice.

Ruger touched her arm. "That's not a good idea."

She jerked away, fire blazing in her eyes. "I have to go. He's going to find me."

Ruger's gaze locked with hers. "Where are you going to go?"

Her gaze skittered around, something deeply unsettled about it. "I don't know. But away from here. The lake. I need to go to the lake."

He grasped both of her arms as she tried to move toward the door. "That's a bad idea, Sarah."

"That's the *only* idea. I have to go. Don't try to stop me!" She tried again to shrug out of his grasp.

But he couldn't let her.

He held on more tightly. "Sarah, you need to listen to me."

Instead, her gaze swung around.

"You don't understand." Her voice cracked. "He's going to kill me. I have to get away."

"He's not going to kill you," Ruger told her. "He's not here. It's just me, and I'll keep you safe."

"No one can keep me safe."

Ruger watched her, his heart pounding in his ears as he saw something begin to break inside her.

Then a sob escaped.

"No one can protect me," she repeated, tears pouring from her eyes.

"Stay here with me. I won't leave you."

As if he'd said the magic words, her bones seemed to turn into jelly.

Ruger pulled her toward him and into an embrace.

"Just breathe in and breathe out," he murmured. "Take deep breaths. Hold them. Then release. It will help get your panic under control."

He felt Sarah's chest rising and falling, the motion becoming steadier with every second.

The best thing he could do right now was simply hold her.

SARAH JERKED HER EYES OPEN, panic stiffening her.

Where was she?

How much time had passed?

She realized she was leaning against Ruger's chest, her arms wrapped around his waist.

They were on the couch, and a fire blazed in front of them. A blanket had been placed around her. Darkness still stared at them from the windows.

She shifted and looked up at Ruger, halfway expecting him to be asleep.

Instead, his eyes were wide and alert.

"Hey." He sounded slightly hoarse as he said the word.

"Hey." She ran a hand through her hair, suddenly feeling self-conscious again. "What happened . . . ?"

As the question left her mouth, everything rushed back to her.

She'd nearly had a panic attack. She'd tried to get out of the house. To go to the lake again.

But Ruger had stopped her.

Nausea formed in her gut at the thought.

What was wrong with her?

She glanced up at him. "I think Charlie should have sent a shrink instead of a security detail."

That got a small smile out of him. "I don't know about that."

"I don't know how you're putting up with me right now. I really don't. I just feel so confused." She ran her hands over her face.

Ruger didn't say anything for a moment, so she spoke instead.

"Bryce once tried to drown me in a lake," she said softly.

As his gaze snapped down to her and his muscles stiffened, Sarah knew she had all of Ruger's attention.

So, she continued, "We lived on the water in St. Louis. You would think that I wouldn't like the water now, but I still do. Anyway, I made him mad one day. We'd been trying to have kids for a while—thank goodness, we didn't bring any children into this mess—but the doctor finally told us that I couldn't get pregnant. However, not long after that, I did."

Ruger shifted, sitting up straighter. "What happened next?"

"Bryce was so excited. But at eight weeks, I miscarried. I was devastated."

She sucked in a deep breath, trying to get her thoughts under control. She hadn't talked about this in a long, long time.

"In public, Bryce seemed like a supportive, concerned husband," she continued. "But as soon as we got back from the hospital, he lashed out. He was furious. He blamed me. He accused me of doing something to lose the baby."

Images of that night flashed back to her until nausea gurgled in her stomach.

"He took me by the hair and dragged me outside to the lake behind our house. He held me under until I confessed that I'd done something to make myself miscarry. Eventually, when I couldn't take any more, I told him he was right. That I hadn't been eating correctly. But it wasn't true. I would *never* harm my baby. I was just desperate to stay alive."

"Was that when you left him?"

She shook her head, feeling foolish to give that answer. "You would think that it would be, right? I know it sounds cliché, but he was so apologetic afterward. I wanted so desperately to believe he was telling the truth. Besides, getting away from him seemed like an impossibility. He'd talked me into quitting my job. I didn't have any of my own money. All the bank accounts were only in his name. He'd isolated me from my friends."

Sarah paused and took in a deep breath.

Then she continued. "I knew he could track my car and my cell phone and trace any purchases made on my credit cards. Even though I tried to save away some cash here and there, I knew the meager amount I'd put away wouldn't get me very far."

"Is that when you found Charlie?"

"No, that wasn't for another three months. Four weeks later, Bryce went into a rage and tried to kill me again."

"I'm so sorry that happened. What set him off that time?"

"There was a function at the hospital, where Bryce was being honored." She paused and swallowed, trying to find enough inner strength to finish. "Bryce always liked to say that 'being on time was as good as being late.' He believed in punctuality, which was ironic considering how long doctors often make their patients wait."

Ruger didn't say anything; he only listened.

"Anyway, I got caught in traffic on the way there,

and I walked in ten minutes after the event had started. He'd wanted me to wear a certain dress, but the zipper caught, and I couldn't wear it. I picked out something else instead. From the moment I walked into the event, I could see the anger simmering beneath his gaze. No one else could. Bryce hid it well. But I knew he was furious with me, that he thought I'd purposefully ruined his big day." She drew in a raspy, shaky breath. "He wouldn't accept my answers. In fact, he didn't speak to me at all during the event. Then when we got home . . ."

"You don't have to finish if you don't want to."

She shook her head and continued. "I want you to know what happened. When we got home . . . he followed me to the bedroom. He told me he was going to draw me a bath. And he did. But I knew something wasn't right." She glanced at her hands, fighting the tears that came to her eyes. "At first, it seemed like he was putting in extra effort by lighting candles and playing soft music. I thought maybe I'd misread him. But then, as soon as he cut off the water, he snapped. He grabbed me. Pushed my head underwater until I couldn't breathe. Just when I thought I was going to die, he'd let me get a breath— only to push me under again."

"Sarah . . ."

The compassion in Ruger's tone was enough to break her. She couldn't let that happen.

"I lost count of how many times he pushed me under. I blacked out. But when I awoke, I was on the bathroom floor. Naked. Wet. Cold. Bryce was outside on the balcony smoking a cigar and laughing on the phone with someone." She drew in a shaky breath. "That's when I knew I had to leave, no matter the cost. I had no proof of what he'd done to me that evening. It would be my word against his. But I didn't know how to escape."

"How did you learn about Vanishing Ranch?"

She let out a deep breath. "I went to visit a women's shelter. I told Bryce I was dropping off some clothes, so he didn't question me. I really don't think he ever considered the idea that I might find the courage to leave him. He was too cocky for that. Anyway, when I got there, the director was in her office and no one else was around. I somehow found the courage to ask her some questions. She seemed to see through me, see that I needed help."

"What happened next?"

"I knew I couldn't deny the abuse. That this could be my one and only chance. So, I told her everything. She said Bryce was powerful and would find me at the shelter, that I couldn't stay there. At first, her words devastated me. Then she handed me a cell phone with one phone number already programmed into it. She told me I could get away, but I would have to leave everything and go no contact with my friends and family. I was willing to do what I needed to do."

"And that's when you called Charlie?"

She nodded. "Before I even walked outside the shelter. At first, I was confused as to why every woman there didn't get this chance. I asked Charlie that, and she told me that not every woman was in the same situation. Some weren't willing to run. Some pressed charges against their husbands or boyfriends. Others just needed financial help until they could get back on their feet."

"I'm glad you called her."

"Charlie helped me fake my death," she said. "I'd been taking sailing lessons. I'd always had a fear of the water, and I told Bryce I wanted to be more comfortable out there. He agreed. But, thanks to Charlie, I picked the perfect bad weather day to go out. My boat drifted to shore without me, and everyone assumed I died, even though my body never washed up."

"What about your family?"

"My dad died when I was two. My mom and I were really never that close. Eventually, she remarried and moved to Florida, but I never heard from her much. The only person I was really concerned about was my brother. He lived about an hour away, and he's married with two kids. I didn't see him often, but I hated for him to think I'd died. But there was no other way."

Sarah glanced out the window again. Even though she couldn't see the lake, she knew it was there. It was always there. Always a reminder of how the water had almost claimed her life—and how it had ultimately given Sarah back her life.

It was one reason why when Charlie had offered her a few different choices for places where she could move, she'd chosen the Kalispell area. She'd seen a picture of this property with the lake and had known it was perfect for her.

Before she could talk about her past anymore, Ruger leaned forward, a serious look in his gaze. "I have a question for you. I've been thinking a lot as you've been resting."

"Okay. Anything you want to know."

His gaze flickered back up to hers. "Do you take any prescription medications?"

She nodded. "I mean, I have a few supplements I take. Other than those, I take something to keep my thyroid hormone levels in a healthy range."

"What time do you take your pills?"

"At night, a little while before I go to bed."

"Have you started taking anything new recently?"

She shook her head. "No, I haven't."

"Do you mind if I see the medicine bottles, even the supplements?"

"Okay." Her eyes narrowed as she tried to figure out what exactly he was thinking.

She'd give him the benefit of the doubt.

But a bad feeling swirled in Sarah's gut as she went to her room and grabbed them.

Ruger studied the bottles, opening them and looking at the pills inside.

"Are you going to tell me what you're thinking?" Sarah watched him carefully, illumination from the fire dancing across her face.

He glanced up at her, locking his gaze with hers. "I'm wondering if someone tampered with your medications."

Her eyes widened as his words hit her. "What? How would somebody do that?"

Ruger shifted his jaw as he thought about it. "I'm not sure if someone snuck inside your place and replaced them or if there's another way. But some medication can make people have what's considered to be psychotic episodes. As a nurse, I'm sure you know that."

Sarah seemed to consider his words a moment before nodding.

"You're right. I never thought about that." She glanced at the pill bottles and frowned. "That could be a possibility, but how will I know for sure?"

He grasped one of the bottles, holding it toward the light as tension stretched across his shoulders. "If you don't mind, I'd like to take one of each of these pills and send them to someone to be tested. Just so we can know for certain."

"Sure, whatever you need to do." But her voice sounded thin, almost fragile.

Ruger closed the bottles and held them in his hand another moment. "That's what I'll do. Tomorrow. I want to know as soon as possible."

Sarah leaned back, seeming to collapse into the couch. She pulled her knees toward her, that dazed look returning to her eyes—but this time, dazed with shock instead of drugs.

"What if that's what has been happening this whole time?" she murmured as she stared into the fire. "What if I'm not losing my mind?"

Ruger's gaze met hers. "I feel like this theory is a solid one, but we won't know for sure until later. Whatever it was that caused you to act that way seems to be out of your system now—for the most part at least. Maybe you should get some rest."

She rubbed her arms. "Getting some rest sounds like a good idea."

Ruger agreed. He only wished Sarah could experience more than a temporary rest.

He wished she could stop living in fear and find some peace.

He would do everything in his power to make that happen.

CHAPTER
TWENTY-ONE

THE REST of the night had been uneventful. For that, Ruger was thankful.

He'd slept on one couch, and Sarah had slept on the other. He figured it would be easier to keep his eye on her that way. He had drifted off into sleep a few times, but it was only once he was sure Sarah was settled.

As per usual, he awoke early to shower and get ready. Today when he wandered back into the living room, Sarah was awake and upright.

Seeing her sitting there with her hair tousled and her eyes sleepy did something unexpected to his heart.

There was no denying that the woman was beautiful. But she was also intriguing. The conversations they'd had showed she possessed a rare depth of character and a truly nurturing spirit. The Bible on her table proved she was a woman seeking after God. The care he'd seen her give to her patients displayed her nurturing spirit.

But those weren't things Ruger should be thinking about right now.

He averted his gaze to his blanket and folded it as he asked her how she was doing.

"I'm . . . okay." She ran a hand through her hair again.

"I'm glad you're already awake. I was hoping you might be able to switch your patients around and not start work until ten. Do you think that's possible?"

She squinted with confusion. "Maybe. I've never actually asked for time off before. Why do you want me to do that?"

"Charlie connected me with a guy who lives about an hour from here. He can test the pills for us. I was going to send them off, but I'd rather know today if possible."

Her gaze seemed to clear as that possibility flit-tered through her. "Of course. Let me make a call and get ready. But I don't think it will be a problem."

Thirty minutes later, they were on the road. They followed Flathead Lake as they headed south, away from Kalispell. Most of the vehicles they passed had fishing poles attached to their bumpers or hunting gear in the back.

If you enjoyed outdoor activities, this was the place to be.

Ruger liked the area more and more the longer he was here. In fact, when this was all over, maybe he'd come back one day to explore these mountains and lakes a little more.

The fresh air was invigorating. The surroundings quiet. The views breathtaking.

Finally, they made a few more turns before pulling up to an old cabin tucked back in the woods.

This wasn't the type of place Ruger had expected.

Caution stiffened his muscles as he approached the front door and raised his hand to knock. Before he could, the door opened, and Thomas Murphy stood there.

The man had the stereotypical qualities of a mad scientist, from his crazy brown curly hair to his thick glasses and his sloppy clothes.

But his smile, at least, seemed affable.

"Ruger, right? Glad you're here. I was expecting you. Did you bring what you were supposed to?" The guy spoke a hundred miles a minute, his words bumping into each other as if he'd had too much caffeine.

Ruger stared at him for a moment.

Then Thomas waved and laughed. "Sorry. Where are my manners? I'm Thomas Murphy. You must be Ruger. Charlie said you were coming." He looked beyond Ruger at Sarah. "And you are?"

"She's Sarah." Ruger didn't want Sarah to give away too many details. Even though Charlie said they could trust this guy, he still wanted to be careful.

Ruger handed Thomas a plastic bag with several pills inside.

Thomas held them up and examined them. "You want to know what these are?"

Ruger nodded. "That's right. I suspect they aren't as they're labeled."

Thomas made a grunting sound as he continued to study them. "That would be unfortunate, now, wouldn't it? I'll see what I can find out."

"Charlie said you might have some answers today."

Thomas made another grunting sound. "Is that what she said? That sounds like Charlie. I make no promises, but I'll see what I can do. Now, I need to get busy, and I'm sure you have things to do also. I'll be in touch."

The next instant, the man closed the door, leaving Ruger and Sarah standing there still trying to catch up from the conversation.

Ruger shrugged at Sarah. "That was memorable."

She let out a little laugh. "That's one way to put it."

But Ruger deeply hoped this guy would be able to provide them with some answers.

Today was Sarah's day to see Mary again.

As soon as the woman answered the door, Sarah knew Mary would be trouble.

Mary glanced at the vehicle where Ruger sat, her eyes gleaming with mischief.

Before Sarah could stop her, Mary pushed her way outside and toward the car. "I have got to meet this guy. He's a hubba hubba hunk of a man."

A hubba hubba hunk?

Sarah felt her cheeks heating as she hurried behind Mary.

But the woman was surprisingly spry. She reached Ruger's car and knocked on the window. Ruger rolled his window down, casting a curious glance at Sarah as he did so.

"I just had to come meet you myself." Mary extended her wrinkled hand. "I'm Mary, and I know Sarah says you're just a friend, but I can read between the lines." She offered an exaggerated wink.

Dread pooled in Sarah's stomach. "Mary, he *is* a family friend."

"If you let a man who looks this good walk away from you, then you're plum crazy, girl."

Sarah wanted to be amused, but she couldn't be. "There's more to a person than how they look."

Mary seemed to rethink her statement. "You're right. I know that. But I can tell by looking at him that he's one of the good ones. A good man who's also a hunk."

A hunk? Did people even use that word anymore?

Sarah's cheeks heated all over again.

"It's nice to meet you, ma'am." Ruger sounded ever so polite.

Which probably meant he was winning even more points with Mary.

Sarah really needed to get the woman inside.

"So, our Sarah is awfully special, isn't she?" Mary placed her hand on Sarah's shoulder. "She comes out to help me even when it's not during working hours. I had this incident where I thought I'd gotten my medications mixed up, and she was the first to come by and give me a hand. Isn't that right, Sarah?"

"I'm just doing what any good nurse would do."

"Well, I've had a whole slew of nurses, and none

of them are like you. You go the extra mile, and you really care. That says a lot about a person."

Sarah felt herself flush. It wasn't often that someone spoke about her so highly. In fact, she'd been so used to Bryce putting her down that Mary's compliment made warmth bubble inside Sarah—warmth she'd cherish for a long time.

Ruger's gaze met Sarah's. "You're right. Sarah is pretty special."

The warmth grew even warmer.

How could he even think that? Especially after how she'd been acting since Ruger had been here.

That wasn't like her.

At one time, she'd been confident and driven and ready to take on the world.

Then she'd gotten involved with the wrong person, and all that had slowly been beaten out of her until she became someone totally dependent on Bryce—socially, emotionally, financially.

As they talked, Sarah's gaze drifted. Mary lived not far from downtown, in a quaint row of houses easily accessible to the area's restaurants and shops.

She sucked in a breath when she saw a familiar face in the distance.

Pierce.

He was driving by in his Mercedes SUV.

Sarah held her breath, something close to fear seizing her.

But he kept driving, passing with just a wave.

Was it just a coincidence that he happened to come past right now?

It could be.

People came in and out of town for a variety of reasons.

But seeing him here still left Sarah with an uneasy feeling.

AS SOON AS Ruger saw Pierce, he tensed, ready to act if needed.

He watched carefully, his shoulders softening when he saw the man continuing by in his car.

Pierce's appearance seemed to have spooked Sarah, and she quickly ushered Mary back inside the house.

Mary . . . Ruger shook his head.

The woman certainly seemed to be a character.

But Ruger had meant his words when he'd agreed with Mary's assessment of Sarah.

There was something very special about her—from her humility, to her concern for people, to the strength she'd shown while going through this awful situation.

Ruger had a feeling that once he figured out what

was going on with her medication, her psychotic episodes would start to make more sense.

As he sat there, his thoughts drifted to Khya, and he frowned.

He'd sensed something broken about her when they'd first met. He'd just thought she needed love and security, and that she'd be fine.

That seemed to work for a long time.

But after Ruger had risen to fame by saving the president, his schedule had been consumed by work. He hadn't been home that much.

Khya had told him she was doing fine and was staying busy with her friends and her job as a teacher.

He'd believed Khya when she'd encouraged him to pursue his dreams, when she'd said this was the opportunity of a lifetime.

That's why he never expected her to take her life and leave the suicide note, pointing to his absence and her loneliness as the main reason.

Guilt still pounded him every time he remembered. Ruger held himself responsible for Khya's death. He should have done more. Should have been able to see what was coming. If he hadn't been on the road so much maybe . . .

His phone rang, snapping him from his dismal thoughts.

It was Thomas.

"I've got something for you," he said. "Can you come back down to my place?"

Ruger shifted in his seat. "You can't tell me over the phone."

"Important conversations should take place in person. Plus, Big Brother is always watching and listening. I don't want him to hear this."

Ruger didn't bother to argue. Instead, he glanced at his watch. He knew Sarah still had two more patients to see.

"We can be there in a few hours," Ruger said. "Does that work?"

"Absolutely. I'll see you then."

Sarah drew in a nervous breath as she and Ruger headed down the road.

Before going to meet Thomas, they stopped by the general store. Ruger was the first to speak as they reached the counter. The clerk there—a young man named Patrick—smiled at Sarah.

As Ruger talked to him, Sarah found a small bin of socks. She picked a pair up, wondering if she could have bought some and not remembered.

But a moment later, Ruger found her and shook

his head. "The clerk said you didn't buy the socks. Some guy came in after you and purchased them. He didn't recognize the man—he was wearing a hat and a sweatshirt."

A chill washed through her. "And then he planted them in my house along with the receipt?"

Ruger shrugged. "That's my best guess."

Sarah didn't like where any of this was going.

Back in the SUV, they headed to Thomas's place.

"At least we know I didn't buy those socks, that I'm not going crazy," Sarah said.

"I'm glad you feel better."

"I'll feel even better after we talk to Thomas. Why can't he tell us about the update on the phone? Does that mean the news is really bad?"

"My impression is that Thomas is eccentric and possibly slightly paranoid. Plus, if he's caught doing some of the stuff he does, he'll go to jail. So, it's generally best if we handle these things face-to-face rather than over the phone where he could be recorded."

"I feel like I'm beside myself as I'm waiting to hear what he found out." Sarah rubbed her neck as she felt her muscles tighten.

Part of Sarah wanted to hear that something had happened with her medication. To have a solid answer to what has been going on. The other part of her feared the implications of that. Because that would mean someone knew what kind of prescription she took. That they'd been manipulative enough to switch out her pills. That they'd known what kind of effect doing so would have on her.

That would take this beyond an accident or an episode and into something much more premeditated.

For now, she just needed to wait to see what Thomas found out.

It felt like hours later when they pulled back up to Thomas's cabin, even though Sarah knew it had only been an hour.

Thomas met them at the door, that same wired look in his eyes. Just as before, he didn't invite them inside. Instead, they stood in the doorway, and he held up some papers.

"You're not taking thyroid medication," he announced.

Sarah's eyes widened. "I'm not?"

He shook his head, looking a little too excited. "No, ma'am, you're not. It's really an opioid containing fentanyl."

"What?" Astonishment gripped Ruger's voice.

"That's right." Thomas nodded. "That's what it is . . . and some people can have crazy reactions to drugs like these. Or even die."

Sarah's head spun. Opioids? How was this even happening?

On a couple of occasions, Bryce had insisted she wasn't well mentally. He'd given her something . . . she hadn't even asked what. But she'd felt as if she were crawling out of her skin. She barely remembered anything that happened afterward. She'd just woken the next morning with a memory lapse.

She remembered Bryce looking rather pleased with himself.

Had he been testing the waters? Seeing how she'd react?

Because he'd never given them to her again.

But Bryce probably knew they'd made her crazy, and that's all he needed to know.

Was he now using that information to his advantage?

"So, our theory was right?" Ruger said. "Someone switched out Sarah's medication?"

"They not only switched them out, but they had these pills especially designed so they'd look like the pills she's actually supposed to take."

Sarah's breath caught. "How is that possible?"

Thomas leaned against the door as if settling in for a long talk. "Have you ever heard about the clandestine labs that produce illegal drugs disguised as other pills?"

"I haven't," Sarah muttered.

"They're out there, and they're big business. If you have the right connections, you can get whatever you want disguised as whatever you need." Thomas paused. "When was the last time you picked up your medication at the pharmacy?"

Sarah felt the blood drain from her face as facts clicked together in her mind. "Four days ago."

CHAPTER
TWENTY-THREE

RUGER FELT anger burning through him.

It took a lot of foresight for someone to go through the trouble of switching out Sarah's medication like that.

How did someone even know what medication she took?

They shouldn't—unless they were either her doctor or her pharmacist. But Sarah had told Ruger that the nurse practitioner in town had prescribed her medication. She said the woman was trustworthy.

Ruger would still look into the woman, but Sarah seemed convinced.

That left the pharmacist.

Which was who he and Sarah were heading to talk to now.

They pulled up in front of a drugstore located in town, and Ruger parked. He wished he could leave Sarah in his SUV and handle this himself, but he couldn't take the risk of leaving her alone—not knowing what he did now.

Instead, they walked into the drugstore and got in line at the pharmacy.

As they did, Ruger watched the man behind the counter. He appeared to be in his mid to late thirties with thinning hair and wire-framed glasses. His pale skin matched the white of his lab coat as he worked on something out of sight.

Finally, it was their turn.

Ruger asked the tech if the pharmacist could meet them at a consult table to the side.

The pharmacist—his nametag read Clayton Barney—sat across from them, a knot of confusion between his eyes. He glanced at Sarah, then Ruger, no sign of recognition in his gaze.

"What can I do to help you?" Clayton folded his hands together as he looked at them.

"What did you do to Sarah's medication?" Ruger got right to the point.

Sweat instantly beaded on the man's forehead. "What are you talking about? Who's Sarah?"

"I'm Sarah."

"We know you messed with her medication and

made it look like she's taking what she's supposed to be taking when, in reality, she's not." Ruger stared the man down.

"That's quite some theory you have there, but I would never do something like that." Clayton glanced around as if to make sure no one else was listening.

"We know you did it, so you need to start talking." Ruger's voice became louder—on purpose as a way of putting pressure on the man.

The pharmacist leaned closer. "Please, keep your voice down."

"I have no intention of remaining quiet about this, even if it means you lose your license. What you did is wrong, and it has serious consequences. If you can't trust your pharmacist, who can you trust?" Ruger said the last part especially loud.

Clayton shushed them before saying through clenched teeth, "I can't talk here."

"Where *can* you talk?"

The man glanced around again before turning back to Ruger and Sarah. "I can meet after work. In an hour at Aspen Grove Park. We can talk there."

Ruger stared at the man, his look letting him know he meant business. "I would really prefer to talk right here, right now."

"I can't do that." Clayton's gaze shifted again

nervously. "If anyone sees me with you, people I love could be in danger."

***

Sarah sat with Ruger on the park bench waiting for Clayton Barney to join them.

In the distance, the sun dipped below the horizon, leaving a wake of gray behind it. Several people enjoyed the playground behind them, most now heading toward their cars since the park closed at sunset.

She still couldn't believe this was all really happening. Everything was such a nightmare.

"I just don't understand all of this," she muttered again. "Why would Clayton target me?"

Ruger's jaw flexed. "It sounds like someone is threatening Clayton that if he doesn't do what they want, someone Clayton loves will be hurt."

"That's just wrong."

"It is, but that's how evil people get what they want."

Sarah's thoughts continued to race. "Who would have threatened him? Bryce?"

Ruger turned toward her, his gaze steady and assessing. "Does Bryce know about your medication?"

"No. I wasn't taking anything for my thyroid when we were married."

His jaw flexed again. "There's no way he should know then. How about Pierce? He's the next suspect in my mind."

"I don't know how he would find out that information—unless he saw me picking up something at the pharmacy." Sarah rubbed her temples, feeling a headache coming on. "I just don't know. But someone wants me to think I'm losing my mind. I can't believe someone would hate me enough to go to these extremes."

"Or someone could want you to run back into their arms." His words hung in the air.

She rubbed her throat, her thoughts racing. "I know I keep bringing up Bryce. But he *is* remarried . . . and he should think I'm dead."

"But if he sees you as a possession, then those things won't matter. Since your body was never found, he could be suspicious. I'm not saying he's our guy. But he could be. I'm trying to keep an open mind."

"I know." Sarah frowned as she glanced around.

This was usually one of her favorite parks. The place was beautiful, with walking trails, a playground, and a lake. But, whereas she usually felt peaceful here, right now she felt anything but.

Why wasn't Clayton here yet?

She glanced at her watch. He was already fifteen minutes late.

"Do you think that he's not going to show?" she asked.

Ruger rubbed his jaw as he glanced up and down the street. "I can't say. But I'm not liking this."

"We can call the pharmacy. See if he's still there."

"Good idea." Ruger pulled out his phone, found the number, and dialed. But after talking to the person on the other end, he discovered that Clayton had left thirty minutes ago.

The pharmacy was only ten minutes from the park, so the man should be here by now.

Sarah's gaze locked with Ruger's. "What are you thinking?"

He frowned. "I'm thinking that Clayton ran."

CHAPTER
TWENTY-FOUR

RUGER FOUND Clayton's home address and headed there with Sarah.

He wasn't letting this go without getting some answers.

Ten minutes later, they pulled up to a mid-century home on the outskirts of town. The first thing he noticed was the expensive car in the driveway—a gray Audi sedan.

He knew that pharmacists made decent money. But still, that car seemed expensive even for someone in that career.

With Sarah by his side, he walked to the front door and knocked.

A moment later, a perky brunette answered, her gaze shifting back and forth between the two of them. "Can I help you?"

"We're sorry to disturb you, ma'am." Ruger tried to carefully choose his words. "But we're looking for your husband. Is he home?"

"Clayton?" She blinked, her smile still plastered in place. "He called about forty minutes ago to say that something popped up and he's running late. I'm not expecting him for another couple of hours. Is there something I could help you with instead?"

Ruger assumed Mrs. Barney had no idea what her husband was doing. When he heard the kids in the background, he knew better than to make a scene here and pull this woman into it.

"No, it's a question specifically for him," Ruger said. "He asked for a home renovation estimate."

The woman's eyes lit. "Home renovation?"

Ruger frowned. "I hope that wasn't supposed to be a surprise."

She clasped her hands together as she drew in an excited breath. "I've been begging him to remodel the kitchen. Is that what this is about?"

Ruger's frown deepened. "I better not say. We can just try back again later."

"You could try tomorrow at the pharmacy maybe. He's supposed to work from eight to five, so it doesn't sound like he's going to be home for much other than sleeping." She grinned and shrugged as if she was used to it.

"I understand." Ruger offered a polite smile. "I'm sorry to disturb you." Before he left, he nodded at the Audi in the driveway. "Nice car, by the way."

The woman beamed at his words. "Clayton just bought it for me. I've always wanted one, and he surprised me for my thirtieth birthday. I couldn't have been happier."

Just what exactly was this guy wrapped up in?

Ruger wasn't sure, but he needed to have his guys check Clayton's bank records.

He'd guess they would find a large deposit within the past week or two.

A deposit that could mean Clayton had been paid to switch out Sarah's medication.

Someone who'd sell their integrity and put someone's life at risk just for cash?

They weren't anyone Ruger considered to be a good guy.

Sarah felt sick to her stomach as she and Ruger rode back to her house.

Was Bryce behind this?

If so, how had he found her?

Even if he was still in St. Louis, he could have somehow paid Clayton off to do this.

But it still didn't make any sense how he'd discovered her new name, her new identity, and her new life. Bryce should think she was dead.

Ruger's voice broke her away from her thoughts. "I'm wondering if it's time to take you away from here and go to Vanishing Ranch."

Vanishing Ranch . . . Sarah had almost enjoyed her time there.

Almost.

The place, located in the desert of Arizona, was a former dude ranch, so it had all the amenities of a former resort. Plus, there were the horses, which Sarah had always loved. Being away from everything had been refreshing in its own way. Yet the process of reinventing herself had been a challenge.

They had to rehearse with her ad nauseam what her new name was and the details of her fabricated past. They went through it so many times so it would come naturally if anyone asked her.

Aimee Daniels had died at Vanishing Ranch, and Sarah Chamberlain had arisen.

She stared out the window a moment. "It's not really fair, you know."

"What's not fair?"

"Bryce is the one who should be in prison right now. He should have lost everything. Instead, he's thriving. He's still practicing medicine. He's remarried. All our friends are still his friends."

"I hear you." Ruger made it clear that he was listening to what she said, but he didn't try to interrupt her by interjecting his own opinions.

People who truly listened were a rare gift.

"I guess I feel like I'm the one who lost everything. Sure, I had the chance to restart with a new life. But it seems like Bryce should have some sort of consequence instead of getting off scot-free."

"Did you ever think about going to the police?" Ruger's voice held no judgment, just curiosity.

Sarah shrugged. "I knew they wouldn't believe me. Bryce was so careful to cover his tracks. He had powerful friends who would vouch for him. Give him alibis. Escaping was really the only option."

Ruger squeezed her arm, leaving his hand there a few seconds longer than necessary.

His touch sent a shiver through her.

She liked the heaviness of his hand. She liked his touch. Liked knowing that someone else was there for her, that she wasn't all alone.

Perhaps Sarah had deprived herself of interpersonal relationships for too long, and without even realizing it, she began to wither. But remaining private and withdrawn had seemed safer than opening herself up to someone again. It definitely seemed safer than opening herself up to the possibility of getting hurt.

"You're right," Ruger finally said as he pulled his hand back. "Life hasn't given you a fair hand. I'm sorry."

As he said the words, Sarah sensed something deeper in their meaning, especially as his voice wavered like it did.

What exactly was going through his mind? Did this have something to do with his wife's suicide? She could only imagine the effect her death had on him.

Sarah wanted to know, but she wasn't sure it would be polite to ask.

Just then, they pulled up to her house, and that seemed a perfect excuse to mind her own business.

TWENTY-FIVE

AS RUGER COOKED DINNER—LEMON butter chicken, his mom's recipe—he admitted to himself that he could no longer deny his growing attraction to Sarah.

She was totally and completely off-limits. He knew that. Any type of relationship was against the Vanishing Ranch policy. And he was a rule follower.

But it had been a long time since he'd felt attracted to a woman.

Not since Khya.

There was just something different about Sarah. About her spirit. About the look in her eyes. About the connection they shared.

Since he'd come to Vanishing Ranch, Ruger had interacted with many of the women there. He'd never, ever felt like this. Nor had he ever considered what it might be like to strike up a romance with someone they were helping.

It didn't feel right to even entertain those ideas.

Besides, it wasn't fair to think of Sarah romantically, especially since she was in such a vulnerable position right now.

So, why couldn't he get Sarah out of his mind?

His thoughts continued to churn as he cooked.

Sarah had gone to clean up and, by the time she returned, dinner was on the table.

After they prayed and began eating, Sarah glanced at him, and he saw the curiosity in her gaze.

She was astute and intuitive. Certainly, she realized he had a history before coming here.

And she'd opened up so much to him about her past and all the painful things that had happened. He had the strange urge to share more with her now.

He cleared his throat, his food suddenly not appetizing. "I think I mentioned earlier that I've been married."

"You did. What was her name?"

"Khya. She was an elementary school teacher."

"Noble profession." Sarah nodded slowly from across the table.

"I agree. A noble profession for a noble woman." He offered a sad smile. "We met in college. She was studying education, and I was majoring in criminal justice. After college, I got a job as a cop and moved to DC. It was all a part of my plan. She married me when I was just a rookie and she was a beginning teacher. Money was really tight for a while."

Sarah listened quietly.

"Four years later, I applied to work for the Secret Service. A year later, I got in. Two years after that, I was assigned to the president's detail. Everything seemed to be going according to plan."

"What happened?"

"I saved the president, as you know, and then, not long after that, I started a new career—one that put me on the road much more often."

He lowered his fork, the feeling in his stomach turning into something close to nausea.

He really didn't talk about Khya much—if at all.

"The truth is that after I saved the president's life, I got a lot of unexpected attention. After all, I was just doing my job, and I never anticipated any praise. Then suddenly, TV stations were calling me and wanting interviews and putting me up on this platform of sorts."

Sarah listened, her gaze on his.

"I was swept up in this whole frenzy of being interviewed. Of being featured on TV specials. Eventually, the Secret Service honorably discharged me. I was getting too much attention to be effective. They offered me an office job, but I knew I wouldn't be happy behind a desk. Besides, other opportunities were knocking. I even got a book deal. I guess you could say I was swept up in the pomp and circumstance of the whole thing."

"Did Khya support you in that?"

"She seemed to." He let out a long breath. "I thought she was doing okay. She gave me her blessing every time I went on tour. But I was gone from home. A lot. Now I realize I was gone too much."

"Did you ever invite her along?" Sarah cut into her chicken and stabbed a piece, raising it toward her mouth. But her full attention was on this conversation.

"I did, but she said it was too hard to get away as a teacher. That she needed to be there for her kids and that subs were great, but they weren't a true replacement for a teacher."

"Makes sense."

"Whenever I saw Khya, she seemed fine. But one day, right after I was interviewed by ABC News, my brother called me. He told me that Khya had over-dosed and was in the hospital."

Sarah gasped. "I'm so sorry."

Ruger barely heard her as he continued to tell his story. He knew if he stopped, he probably wouldn't start again. "I raced to her side but, by the time I arrived, it was too late. She was gone. I had no idea she was even struggling, which made me feel like the worst husband ever. How could I not have seen that?"

"I'm sorry she didn't share it with you."

"It wasn't her fault. It was mine. I should have done more . . ."

Sarah reached across the table and squeezed his hands. "Just because you feel guilt doesn't mean it's justified. What you're dealing with is very common. It's part of being a suicide survivor. But beating yourself up will do no good. Sure, it's part of the grieving process. It's something everyone in your shoes goes through."

When he said nothing, she continued.

"Maybe it makes you feel better to beat yourself up. Maybe you feel as if you deserve it. But none of that is true. Suicide is tragic—for the person whose life is gone and for those who are left behind. I know it's hard, but you have to forgive yourself. Even though it may not feel like it, you deserve to move on."

"You sound like you know."

She shrugged. "Not personally. Not really. But I took a whole seminar on it. It helped while working in the ER because sometimes we had people come in who . . ." She didn't finish her statement.

He appreciated Sarah's touch. Her compassion.

He opened his mouth to let her know how easy she was to talk to when his phone vibrated.

It was a sensor letting him know that something had triggered the security camera outside.

He rose and locked his gaze with Sarah's. "Stay here. If you don't hear from me in ten minutes, call the police."

Her eyes widened, and she looked as if she wanted to argue. Instead, she nodded.

Ruger grabbed his gun and started toward the door.

Cautiously, Ruger stepped outside into the nighttime air.

As he did, he glanced around, looking for a sign of anyone who might be hiding.

He'd checked the security camera footage.

A figure dressed in black was outside of Sarah's house.

Was it Bryce?

He didn't think the man was the type to do his

own dirty work. But it was anyone's guess at this point.

Staying near the edge of the house, he surveyed the area.

The darkness made it hard to see. His eyes hadn't adjusted yet, which put him at a disadvantage.

As he reached the corner of the house, he paused and glanced around.

He still didn't see anything.

He scanned the woods in the distance. Black abysses stared at him from between the trees. The moonlight, which had previously offered its guidance, now remained concealed behind clouds, making everything even darker.

Had those guys who'd been camping near the property come back?

Ruger didn't think so, but he needed to be sure.

Someone was definitely out here.

He walked the perimeter of the house before pausing at another corner.

As he leaned to see if anyone was there, something hard came down on his head.

Pain spread through him as everything went black.

CHAPTER
TWENTY-SIX

SARAH FELT beside herself as she stood against the hallway wall and waited.

Where was Ruger? Was he okay?

She tried to pull up the app on her phone so she could see the security footage also. But something went wrong, and it wasn't working. Maybe it had something to do with the fact that her hands were trembling. Anxiety had her rattled.

She closed her eyes. *Please, Lord, be with Ruger. Protect him. Keep him safe.*

She wanted to move to the window. To check outside.

But she didn't dare.

Instead, she pressed herself against the wall.

Images of the last time she'd seen Bryce replayed in her mind.

He'd left for work. Had kissed her cheek and told her to have fun sailing.

That evening they were supposed to go to a family dinner at his parents' house. He'd already picked out an outfit for her to wear.

She'd known if she said or did anything wrong, that she'd pay.

She couldn't bear the thought of going through that again. The thought of Bryce smoking a cigar and laughing while she lay on a cold tile floor suffering and nearly dead made her feel ill.

Her throat constricted as she remembered the pain she'd experienced. As she remembered her life flashing before her eyes.

Dr. Bryce Daniels knew how to heal. But he also knew how to inflict pain to its fullest extent.

That was exactly what he'd done.

Sarah tried to suck in a breath, but her lungs felt as if they'd filled with cement.

She couldn't stay here while knowing Ruger could be in danger.

But she'd promised him she would. That she would call the police if he wasn't back in ten minutes.

She glanced at her watch.

Six minutes had passed.

Could she really wait four more minutes?

She wasn't sure.

That's when she heard something outside.

Was Ruger coming back?

Or was the intruder trying to get in?

As quickly as the darkness had closed over Ruger, he jerked his eyes open.

He wasn't going down that easily.

He felt the blood running down his face, warm and sticky.

But as his gaze focused, he realized he was still outside.

The man in black, he remembered.

Ruger looked up.

Pierce stood in front of him, a shovel in his hands as he faced Ruger.

"You don't want to do that," Ruger growled as he lay sprawled on the ground.

"I think I do." Pierce raised the shovel and swung it toward Ruger again.

Ruger quickly rolled out of the way and popped to his feet. His shoulder caught the man in his abdomen, and Pierce let out a grunt of pain.

The next instant, Ruger tackled him to the ground. Once he'd subdued the man, he flipped

Pierce over facedown. Ruger pinned his arms behind him and held him against the ground until some of his fight faded.

"You done yet?" Ruger asked.

"You're not going to get away with this," Pierce growled through clenched teeth.

What was this guy talking about?

Ruger wasn't sure. But he needed to find out.

"You and I need to talk," Ruger muttered.

"It sounds like we do."

As Pierce began to struggle against Ruger again, Ruger released him.

The man scrambled to his feet and reached for the shovel.

Before he could grab it, Ruger drew his gun and locked his gaze with Pierce. "I wouldn't do that if I were you."

Pierce's eyes widened, and he raised his hands. "Don't do anything stupid."

"I could say the same for you." Ruger nodded toward the door. "Now walk."

SARAH HEARD the doorknob turn and held her breath as she waited to see who would come inside.

She clutched her phone in her hands as if it were a weapon.

But it wasn't.

She could call the police but, by the time she started to dial, it would be too late.

She knew that.

But she didn't know what else to do.

She hated how fear had frozen her.

The door flung open.

Two figures stepped in.

Ruger . . .

He was okay!

But blood ran down the side of his face, and his

eyes looked hard and angry as he aimed his gun toward the man with him.

Sarah's gaze focused on the other guy.

It wasn't Bryce.

It was . . . Pierce.

Pierce?

What was he doing here?

Sarah had the urge to rush toward Ruger, to make sure he was okay—especially when she saw the blood on him.

But she sensed she shouldn't get that close—not while he held Pierce at gunpoint.

"Sarah . . . Are you okay?" Pierce rushed, his entire body tense and looking ready to spring.

She rubbed her arms and remained where she was—a safe distance away. "I'm fine. What are you doing here?"

Ruger shoved him forward until Pierce practically fell into one of the dining room chairs.

He perched precariously there as he stared up at her. "I had to check on you."

What was he talking about?

Sarah tilted her head. "Check on me? Why did you need to check on me?"

Pierce scowled at Ruger. "Because something isn't right with this guy. I know he's supposed to be a family friend, but he seems to feel ownership over you. Ever since he came to town, I've been worried about you, Sarah."

"Pierce . . . there's no need to worry about me. I'm just fine." It seemed ironic Sarah was saying those words, considering everything that had happened.

"What were you doing lurking outside the house?" Ruger demanded as he tucked his gun away and stood in front of Pierce. "Why not just knock on the front door?"

Pierce's gaze narrowed even more as Ruger moved in front of Sarah. "It's like I told you. I've been worried about Sarah. I didn't knock because I knew you probably wouldn't answer the door."

"What made you think I was in any danger?"

"I saw you walking barefoot down the road at night a few days ago. I tried to talk to you, but it seemed like you were in a trance or something. When I tried to help, you screamed and ran back to your house. I didn't know what was happening. I tried knocking on your door, but you didn't answer."

Her cheeks heated. She hadn't even realized she'd done that. However, that explained the dirt she'd found on her feet.

"Then this guy showed up." Pierce scowled at Ruger again. "He seems possessive. I mean, he's driving you around. Answering questions for you. Not leaving your side."

"He's not possessive," Sarah said. "He's *protective*."

She believed those words. She understood there was a fine line between possessive and protective, but, in her gut, she sensed where Ruger fell.

He was nothing like Bryce. Nothing.

Sarah rubbed her arms, feeling the goosebumps there. She stepped to the side so she could see around Ruger and drive home the truth with Pierce. "Pierce . . . I appreciate your concern, but I'm fine. I promise."

Pierce's gaze shifted back and forth between Ruger and Sarah as if he were trying to figure out if he believed her.

"I've got things under control. You need to leave." Ruger stepped closer until he towered over the man. "I've been nice this time. But next time, I may not be."

"Is that a threat?" Pierce bristled in his seat.

"It's not a threat. It's the truth. You have two minutes to leave before I call the police to report an assault." Ruger pointed at his head where blood still dripped from his wound.

"Fine." Pierce stood and peered around Ruger at Sarah. "If you need anything, call me."

She nodded, almost reluctantly. Pierce seemed to have good intentions. She'd certainly wished someone had been watching out for her when she was with Bryce. But either no one noticed or everyone turned a blind eye.

With one last glance at Ruger, Pierce left.

She hoped they'd put his worries at ease, and he'd leave her alone now.

Ruger could hardly believe how this was playing out.

Could hardly believe Pierce had been lurking outside because he was worried about Sarah.

He still didn't trust the man. Didn't trust that he wasn't behind some of those incidents.

Sarah stepped closer, peering at Ruger's injury, and gently touched the side of his face.

When Ruger flinched at the feel of her fingers against his skin, she withdrew as if she'd been scolded.

She quickly composed herself. "I need to get you cleaned up."

"I'm fine . . ." Yet Ruger knew he wasn't fine. He could feel the blood—partway dried now and partway still gooey—sticking to the side of his face.

"I'm a nurse, and I say you're not fine. Sit down, and I'll be right back." She rushed into the bathroom and returned with the first aid kit.

Ruger tried to remain stoic as she took a damp

cloth and began washing the blood from his face. "I'm sure it looks worse than it is."

Sarah ignored him. "How did this happen?"

"When I walked around the corner, Pierce hit me with a shovel."

She let out a soft gasp. "I'm so sorry that happened. I don't know what he was thinking . . ."

There she went again, apologizing for things she wasn't responsible for. No doubt, it was a bad habit, one that had been born during her time with Bryce. Ruger had seen it time and time again.

"It's not your fault," Ruger said.

"I know, but . . ." A frown tugged at her lips.

It sounded like they were both carrying guilt not belonging to them, yet they couldn't seem to shrug it off, no matter how hard they tried. Was that their bond? Misplaced guilt?

Bryce had clearly made Sarah feel like everything was always her fault.

Whereas Ruger's guilt was deserved.

He frowned, and Sarah must have thought she'd done something because more regret filled her gaze.

"This might sting." She put ointment on some gauze and dabbed his cut.

Ruger was all too aware of how close she was.

All too aware of how clean and fresh she smelled from her earlier shower.

All too aware of how attracted to her he was.

"This is a change, huh?" Her voice sounded thin. "Me taking care of you instead of vice versa."

"I guess it is."

"You could use some stitches, but I might be able to use some butterfly bandages." She frowned again as she studied his wound.

"Let's try those first." He didn't want to make a bigger deal of this than it was.

Sarah took the bandages from the packages and tenderly pressed them on his forehead, just near his hairline.

Each touch sent shivers through him. Made him want to reach out and feel her soft skin against his fingertips.

He pressed his eyes closed, drawing on every ounce of his self-control to keep his hands to himself.

When he'd taken this assignment, fighting attraction to the woman he was protecting was the last challenge he'd expected to encounter.

CHAPTER
TWENTY-EIGHT

WHEN SARAH REALIZED that Ruger had put his life on the line for hers, something had flooded her heart.

Something more than gratitude and appreciation.

Something more like . . . affection.

Against all the odds, she was beginning to have feelings for this man.

She wasn't looking for love or romance.

Yet here it was.

The closest thing she had felt to it in years, at least—although, what she and Bryce had wasn't love. She'd thought it was at first. But love was supposed to be patient and kind, to be slow to anger and quick to show mercy.

Bryce had been none of those things.

As she put the last bandage on Ruger's injury, she gently ran her finger across his forehead.

Her hand seemed to take on a mind of its own, and she continued trailing her finger down his face. Along his barely there beard. To his neck, where she paused.

Ruger looked up at her, something intriguing in his gaze.

Her heart beat at a steady but quick tempo—a fact she was painfully aware of. Her every move-ment—Ruger's also—seemed to consume her focus.

She wasn't sure what came over her.

But Sarah leaned down and pressed her lips against his. She needed to let him know how much she appreciated him.

But really, this wasn't about logic at all.

Instead, an unseen force seemed to draw them together.

Ruger felt it too. She could see it in his eyes.

He reached for her and wrapped his arms around her waist then he pulled her into his lap. He reached for her neck and drew her closer as the kiss deepened.

But as quickly as it started, Ruger pushed her away.

He stood and turned his back to her, raking a

hand through his hair as he let out a deep, almost agony-filled breath.

Rejection washed over her, and her cheeks heated.

"I'm sorry." She pressed her fingers over her lips, Ruger's taste still lingering there.

What had she been thinking?

Hadn't she made enough bad decisions to last a lifetime?

Ruger's heart raced along with his thoughts. What just happened?

He knew he'd been toeing a dangerous line with his attraction to Sarah. But he'd never intended on acting on it.

Even though Sarah had initiated that kiss, his desire had kicked in. And he'd felt powerless to stop them—at least, for several seconds.

As he glanced at Sarah now, he saw the rejection on her face.

His shoulders softened as he realized what was probably going through her head.

"Sarah . . ." He started to reach for her but dropped his hand.

Touching her probably wasn't a good idea right now.

She raised her palm toward him and shook her head. "You don't have to explain. I'm so sorry. I don't know what came over me. I'm not usually—"

"Sarah . . ." Ruger's voice sounded low and husky as he stepped closer. "Don't apologize."

She glanced up at him, confusion in her gaze. But she didn't say anything. She only waited for him to continue.

"I would love nothing more than to pursue this," he pointed between the two of them, "more. But I can't. Not while I've been charged with guarding you. Do you understand?"

"I get it. We crossed a professional boundary that we shouldn't have."

He nodded, again reaching for her. But this time, he didn't drop his hand. Instead, he used the side of his palm to wipe the small trickle of moisture coming from her eyes.

Then he slowly lowered his arm back down to his side and willed it to stay there. "This isn't the right time. I need to stay focused on helping you. I can't allow myself to get distracted by my feelings."

She stared at him, a strange emotion swirling in her gaze, until she finally nodded. "I know."

"Good." His voice sounded at a whisper. "But when this is all over . . . let's revisit this conversation again, okay?"

"Okay."

"For now, I think it's best if we both get some sleep."

Sarah didn't argue.

But Ruger's throat burned as he took a step away from her and remembered with painful clarity just how wonderful that kiss had been.

TWENTY-NINE

AS SOON AS he knew that Sarah had drifted to sleep, Ruger picked up his phone to call Charlie.

He needed to check in with her every day anyway, but he especially wanted to let her know about the developments of today.

Minus the kiss.

That had *clearly* been a mistake, one that he wouldn't make again—not while on duty.

Maybe not ever.

Not after Khya.

Ruger had proven he wasn't fit to be a husband. He didn't deserve to find happiness again—not after Khya had suffered as she did. He needed to keep that at the forefront of his thoughts.

Charlie listened as Ruger gave her the update on the medication and Pierce.

Then he asked, "Do you think I should take Sarah back to Vanishing Ranch?"

"It definitely seems as if danger is rising. I don't want to keep her there if it seems she'll get hurt."

"I don't either, and something is definitely going on here. However, I'm not sure that she wants to go back to Vanishing Ranch only to start a brand-new life again somewhere else."

Charlie didn't say anything a moment before finally agreeing. "I can see where she's coming from. Switching identities . . . it's not easy."

"I can only imagine."

She let out a long breath. "Let's give it another day. If we have to bring her back here to recalculate before sending her back to Kalispell, then that's what we'll do. I'll make it happen. As you know, we never force anyone to do something against their will, even if we don't agree with their decisions."

"That's only smart." People needed to be responsible for their own choices. Being forced into doing something would only make them run or feel resentment.

"So, we wait until tomorrow. Things have slowed down here—not much, but slightly. I'm recruiting some new hires to help with our workload. But as soon as your instinct says you guys need to get out of there, you leave. I'll figure out a way to get you back here. I promise you that."

Ruger nodded as he frowned. "Thank you."

"And, by the way, I had to send Mateo to work another assignment. It just happens to be near St. Louis. He confirmed with his own eyes that Dr. Bryce Daniels has been there and is currently there. I know that's not surprising since the good doctor has the money to hire people to do his dirty work. But Mateo *did* overhear him telling a man he's about to go on a family vacation out west."

Ruger's muscles bristled. He didn't like the sound of that.

"Good to know," he muttered.

"I'll also look into those financials and see if this pharmacist recently got a big payout. I have a feeling he did. I should be able to let you know something by tomorrow."

"That sounds good. Thanks."

"And, Ruger," Charlie's voice turned firm, "in the meantime . . . stay safe."

The next morning, Sarah was still thinking about that kiss.

She couldn't help but replay it in her mind.

Then the kiss had ended, and she recoiled with regret at *that* memory.

Yet Ruger had explained himself. Even though Sarah understood his thought process, that didn't stop her from feeling self-conscious and slightly embarrassed. Kissing him had been so out of character for her. Her emotions were wreaking havoc on her, it seemed.

Sarah had to stop herself from apologizing again. Right now, he was driving her to the third patient's house for the day.

The two of them hadn't said much to each other this morning.

It was almost a relief when he pulled up to the house, and she climbed out.

Maybe some space from him would be a good thing.

She walked to her patient's door and punched in a code on the keypad there.

Dorothy Stevenson had trouble walking, so the home healthcare agency had been given the code to let themselves inside at the appointed time.

Dorothy had a stroke not long ago, and she still had trouble communicating and moving. However, she insisted on staying in her home and not going to a rehab facility.

Sarah's agency got a lot of people like that, and

Sarah almost couldn't blame them. If she was recovering from a health emergency, she would want to be at home where she was comfortable also. That was the beauty of home healthcare.

She closed the door behind her and strode inside, heading toward the living room where Dorothy always sat in her oversized navy-blue recliner. She plastered on a grin, knowing the importance of having a cheery attitude.

Grumpy nurses only slowed recovery. It was one of the lessons she had learned in nursing school.

Usually, Dorothy offered a half grin as soon as she saw her.

But today, a new look captured Dorothy's eyes.

"Is everything okay?" Concern instantly rushed through Sarah.

What if Dorothy had experienced some type of medical episode? She'd sounded okay when Sarah had called to confirm their appointment earlier this morning.

But, right now, something felt off.

Dorothy looked at her, opened her mouth to say something.

No words came out.

Had the woman had another stroke?

Sarah started to rush toward her, to check her vitals.

Before she could, someone lunged from the hallway. In the blink of an eye, a thick hand covered Sarah's mouth. An arm clamped against her chest, locking her arms against her.

Sarah struggled against the figure. But it was no use.

She couldn't move her arms.

No screams would escape.

Was this one of Bryce's guys?

If it was, then Sarah needed to think fast . . . not only for her own sake but for Dorothy's.

RUGER WAITED in his car for Sarah to emerge.

He really wished he could go inside with her at each patient's house, but he understood that, for confidentiality reasons, he could not.

Instead, he spent his time surveying the area to make sure nothing suspicious was happening around them. He also made a few phone calls and did some research on his phone.

Charlie had already called this morning and confirmed that the nurse practitioner who'd written the prescription for Sarah was clean, with no criminal history or unusual financial activities.

However, a fifty-thousand-dollar deposit had been made into Clayton Barney's bank account just last week.

That clarified to Ruger that someone powerful was behind this.

Someone like Bryce.

Sarah's ex made the most sense.

But Ruger hadn't completely ruled Pierce out either. The man rubbed him the wrong way. Plus, he lived in town, close enough to keep an eye on Sarah—which the man was apparently keen on doing.

At the thought, Ruger touched the bandage at his forehead.

What a night . . .

That kiss with Sarah fluttered through his mind again. He thought about how sweet she smelled. How soft she felt.

How electricity had zinged up his spine and lit his brain up with possibilities of a future together.

Then an image of Khya filled his mind.

Even though on the surface it might seem like Khya and Sarah were alike, they really weren't.

Besides . . . was Sarah right? Was it time to let go of that guilt? To forgive himself?

He'd been carrying the burden of Khya's death for so long. Punishing himself by trying to keep any kind of happiness at arm's length.

What would his life look like if he could let those things go?

Before those thoughts could go any further, a noise caught his ear.

He straightened.

Something almost sounded like a crash.

Had that come from inside the house?

Ruger sprung from his vehicle and rushed toward the front door. He twisted the door handle, thankful it was unlocked.

Then he grabbed his gun and barged into the house.

As soon as he stepped inside, he saw a man in a black mask struggling with Sarah.

"Get your hands off her!" Ruger raised his gun.

Then he spotted the oxygen tank in the corner, near the recliner where an older woman sat.

He couldn't fire his Glock in here. The bullet could cause an explosion.

The man seemed to know that. Even though he wore a mask, Ruger sensed his smirk.

The man's arm snaked around Sarah's neck. He clutched a knife in his hand, the blade dangerously close to Sarah's skin as he dragged her backward.

Beyond them, Sarah's patient sat in a recliner with wide, fearful eyes as she watched the whole thing.

This situation could turn even uglier quickly.

Ruger couldn't let that happen.

He crept closer. "I said, let go of her."

The man—bulky and covered in black from head to toe, other than his eyes—glared back at Ruger. "I heard you. You're the one who needs to step back. To walk away. Do that, and no one will be hurt."

"I don't think so."

Ruger really wished he could use his gun right now.

But pulling that trigger would be bad news.

Sarah stared at him, panic in her gaze—panic Ruger wished he could erase.

"I'm going to walk out of here." The man stepped toward the back door, Sarah still in tow. "Don't try anything."

"You're not going to walk out of here with Sarah." Ruger bristled as he prepared himself to act. "I won't let that happen."

The man pressed the knife harder into Sarah's throat until she gasped.

Then he sneered, "I don't think you have much choice."

Sarah froze with fear.

This man was going to kill her, wasn't he?

And right in front of Ruger and Dorothy.

Panic pulsed through her as her thoughts raced.

There had to be something she could do.

Yet the prick of the knife seemed to shut her down, to remind her that one move on this man's part could end her life. One wrong move on her part could also send that blade deep into her skin, into an artery.

Ruger stepped toward the man. "Let her go."

"No. You need to move out of my way before my knife slips."

Sarah listened closely to the man's voice—as much as she could between the overwhelming sound of her heart pounding in her ears.

She didn't think she recognized his voice.

Whatever happened, she couldn't leave with this man. If she did, she felt certain she'd never be seen alive again.

The masked man pulled her toward the door as Ruger watched, his eyes narrow and his muscles hard.

At once, Sarah remembered one of the self-defense moves she'd been taught at Vanishing Ranch. The course had been part of her time there—an important part.

She lifted a quick prayer for courage as she gathered her strength.

Then she jammed her elbow into the man's abdomen.

The motion took him by surprise.

Seeing a brief window of opportunity, Sarah squirmed. She dropped until she was out of his arms.

He tried to grab her again when Ruger charged toward him.

He met the guy in three strides, and his fist collided into the man's jaw.

The man in black grunted.

Sarah scrambled out of the way, sensing the coming fight. She hurried toward Dorothy, desperate to protect the woman.

The next instant, the man lunged toward Ruger.

Ruger bent forward, his shoulder catching the man's midsection, and throwing the attacker over his shoulder.

The intruder crashed onto Dorothy's coffee table, smashing it into pieces.

As Ruger grabbed the man's arm and twisted it, the knife clattered from his hand.

Sarah jumped forward, kicked the weapon across the room, and then hurried back to Dorothy.

Now it was man against man—a fair fight, in theory.

But Sarah instinctively knew the man in black would be no match against Ruger.

She was right.

In one move, Ruger flipped the guy onto his

stomach and pinned his hands behind him. Ruger pressed his knees into the man.

The man let out another grunt but didn't move.

He couldn't.

"Who are you?" Ruger demanded, his voice hard. He jerked the man's mask off, but an unfamiliar face stared back.

Sarah had never seen him before.

"None of your business," the man grumbled.

"I think it is. Who are you?" Ruger repeated.

Before the man could answer, sirens sounded outside.

The police? They were here?

Sarah sucked in a breath.

She had been careful not to get the police involved.

She feared they'd ask too many questions. That they'd figure out who she really was. That word would get back to Bryce somehow.

But when she glanced at Dorothy, she saw the phone in the woman's hand and realized who had called 911.

CHAPTER
THIRTY-ONE

RUGER SNEERED at the man in front of him.

He heard the sirens. Knew the police were here.

Even though Sarah's patient had only been trying to look out for them, the police were the last people Ruger wanted involved right now. They might ask too many questions.

Ruger pressed his knees harder into the man's back, knowing he was making it difficult for the guy to breathe.

He only had a couple of minutes to get answers so he repeated, "Who are you?"

The man winced before saying through clenched teeth, "It doesn't matter."

"Who hired you?" This guy wasn't acting on his own. He was a puppet for someone else. Ruger was sure of it.

The man still said nothing.

Ruger leaned closer and growled, "You're going to want to talk."

"You can't make me."

Ruger could think of several ways he could make him.

Just then, four officers flooded the house.

Ruger kept the man's arms pinned behind him as he turned to the closest one. "I heard a crash and came inside. That's when I discovered this man in the house. He'd put a knife to the nurse's throat, so I subdued him."

"We'll take him from here." The officer pulled out some cuffs.

Another officer corroborated the story with Sarah and her patient while two others checked out the rest of the house.

As the man was hauled outside to a police car, Ruger glanced at Sarah. Thank God, she was okay, that her only injury was a small line of blood on her neck from where the knife had pricked her.

That could have turned out so much worse.

What if Ruger hadn't heard something crash inside? What if the man had used that knife to kill Sarah?

His muscles tightened at the thought.

He didn't like where all this was going.

But, right now, he knew they'd have to head down to the station to give their statements.

Ruger prayed that Sarah's true identity wasn't revealed in the process.

⸻

Ruger's jaw continued to twitch as he waited to go to the police station.

Sarah had checked Dorothy to make sure the incident hadn't raised her blood pressure too much. Ruger could see she was worried about the woman, but Dorothy appeared to be fine. Just in case, the head nurse—Sarah's boss—had arrived to sit with Dorothy and monitor her vitals.

Dorothy's family had also been called, and they were on their way. The woman would need someone to keep an eye on her after the frightful experience.

Detective Alan Jefferson, who'd be handling the investigation, had also shown up at Dorothy's. The man was in his forties and had droopy eyelids that covered bloodshot eyes.

Sarah had told Ruger that she'd seen the man a couple of times in town and everyone seemed to think highly of him.

Ruger hoped she was right and that he was a

standup guy. This investigation, in the wrong hands, could be ugly.

As he and Sarah stood outside, waiting for the cue to leave, snippets of the detective's conversation with the man in black drifted through the air. The two men stood by a squad car, about to head to the station.

Ruger strained to listen.

He needed to know who this man was.

"Do you know this man?" The detective held up a photo. "Clayton Barney?"

"How am I supposed to know who that guy in the picture is?" the intruder barked.

"We're investigating his disappearance. He just so happened to disappear just as you appeared. I don't think that's coincidental."

"I don't know him." Defiance hardened the man's voice.

"What about Dorothy? Why were you in her house? What exactly were you planning on doing?"

The man went quiet.

Certainly, the guy realized if he said he didn't know Dorothy either that he'd only look more suspicious. Then he'd have to confess that he'd targeted Sarah. That would only lead to more questions.

The man's best bet was to make it seem like this was a random crime that had spiraled out of control.

"Mr. Barney's car was found abandoned on the side of the road with blood inside," Jefferson said. "Upon examination of the vehicle, we don't believe he was involved in an accident, but instead that something criminal took place."

Sarah sucked in a breath beside Ruger when she heard that update.

That was news to him also.

What exactly had happened to Clayton? Had he made a deal with the devil and ultimately paid the price?

Before Ruger could eavesdrop anymore, an officer came for them and said he'd follow them to the station.

Ruger knew when they arrived that the police would separate them to make sure that their stories matched. He'd been expecting it.

But he didn't like being away from her.

Especially in light of everything that had happened.

CHAPTER
THIRTY-TWO

AN HOUR LATER, Sarah carefully gave Detective Jefferson a rundown of the events that happened at Dorothy's house. Her mind raced as she tried to keep all the details straight.

That was the hard part about living a lie.

You had to remember what your lies were. Otherwise, people would realize the truth.

Sarah had never been one who wanted a complicated life.

But that was exactly what she had right now.

At the start of their conversation, she'd given Detective Jefferson her license, and she'd seen him run it through the system.

To say she was on edge would be an understatement.

"So, you're from Texas?" Detective Jefferson

started, leaning back in his seat and almost appearing too casual.

His laptop computer was in front of him, and, on occasion, he typed something into it.

Was he looking into her background? What reason would he have for doing so? If he was just taking her statement, then she shouldn't be a suspect.

But what if she was?

Her throat tightened.

"Great state," the detective offered.

"It is. The best, if you ask me." Sarah had been well-versed in what to say. At Vanishing Ranch, they'd gone over these details mercilessly. She only hoped she remembered all of it now that it mattered the most. "There's nothing quite like those Friday night lights out there in those small towns."

"Absolutely." He continued to look at his computer. "So, you moved here a couple of years ago?"

"Sure did. Just needed the change, I suppose. Bad breakup, you know?" Sarah shifted, already weary of the chitchat. "If you don't mind me asking, who was that guy in Dorothy's house?"

"Dorothy said he barged into her house about fifteen minutes before you showed up. He threatened her, said if she indicated to anyone he was there, he'd kill her. When he heard you come in, he hid."

"Did he want to rob her?" Sarah thought she knew the answer, but she wanted to know what the detective thought.

"We're trying to figure that out." He shifted as he shrugged. "He could have felt threatened when you came in. There's no reason anyone would come after you, right?"

Was the question pointed? Or casual?

Sarah wasn't sure.

Playing it safe, she shrugged. "None that I can think of. I'm just a home healthcare nurse. I usually don't make people mad."

"Of course. Did he say anything that gave you an indication of his intentions?"

The scene flashed back into her mind. *I'm going to walk out of here. Don't try anything.* She remembered the knife at her throat. She could still feel where the blade had pricked her skin.

But it didn't feel safe to tell the detective those things.

Instead, she swallowed. "Not really."

"Why did he grab you?"

Sarah shrugged. "I suppose Dorothy wasn't a threat, and I was. Then Ruger came in . . . it's all a blur, really."

Jefferson leaned back again and nodded slowly.

"All right, thanks for your patience, Ms. Chamberlain. I'm sorry you had to go through this."

Sarah let out a breath.

She'd done it. She'd gotten through giving her statement without stumbling too much.

But Sarah had a feeling this whole ordeal wasn't over yet.

***

Detective Jefferson stared at Ruger, questions in his gaze. Sarah had left the room ten minutes ago, and he'd been called in. The look Sarah had given him indicated her time with the detective had gone well.

He hoped he could say the same when he was finished.

"So, you're an old family friend?" Detective Jefferson asked.

Ruger wasn't sure what to think of this guy yet. But he needed to make the detective think he was Sarah's friend—or at least a professional colleague.

"That's right." Ruger nodded. "From Houston. Sarah's parents and my parents go way back."

The detective tilted his head. "Do you always drive Sarah around when you come?"

Ruger knew why the man might be suspicious, and he needed to put the man's questions at bay.

"I'm not sure if Sarah mentioned this to you or not, but she was in a serious car accident a couple of years ago. It left her pretty shaken up. Last week, she was almost run off the road while coming home from work. She said the other driver just wasn't paying attention. Anyway, it brought back a lot of bad memories. She called and asked if I'd visit. I had some time off, so I took a road trip to see her. She feels better right now if I'm the one driving her."

Detective Jefferson nodded as if that made sense. "How long are you in town for?"

Ruger shrugged. "Probably only a few more days. But we'll see."

The detective leveled his gaze. "I looked into your background—just as a matter of routine. You used to be Secret Service, is that correct?"

Ruger's throat tightened. "That's right."

Jefferson let out a grunt as if impressed. "Nice. I even read up on you some. Saw that you were the one who saved the president. Kudos. What doesn't make sense to me is how you went from that to being here."

Now Ruger was starting to get uncomfortable. "Like I said, Sarah and I are old family friends."

The detective nodded again. "And you have no idea why this person might go after Sarah? Or was it

Sarah? Maybe it was you. Could this have something to do with your time in the Secret Service?"

His throat tightened. "The guy didn't look familiar. Besides, I've been out of the Secret Service for a while, and I'm unsure who would come after me after all this time. Plus, I didn't tell anybody I was coming here."

The detective narrowed his gaze as he observed Ruger. "So, you think it has to do with Ms. Chamberlain?"

Ruger knew he needed to be careful so he wouldn't cast any doubt on Sarah either. The last thing he wanted was for the detective to go digging deeper into her background.

"I'm telling you that I have no idea. Sarah is a beautiful woman. This guy could've seen her on the street and decided he wanted her, for all I know."

The detective didn't say anything.

Ruger stared at Jefferson another moment, wondering exactly what this guy was thinking. That's when he decided to ask him.

"Why do I feel like I'm a suspect?" Ruger asked. "Like I'm being interrogated even though I'm one of the victims here?"

His words seemed to snap the detective out of interrogation mode. "Of course, you're not a suspect. We're just trying to find out some answers."

Ruger stared at him. "Is there anything else you need from me then?"

Detective Jefferson straightened the files in front of him. "I don't believe so."

Ruger stood, his chair legs scraping against the floor. "Then I'll be going."

And he would be.

As soon as he found Sarah.

RELIEF WASHED through Sarah when the cops said they could leave.

Ruger also looked thankful. But neither spoke until they were headed down the road in Ruger's SUV.

It was only then that either of them seemed to relax—and, even then, they didn't relax much.

"Do you think they're suspicious that you're not really Sarah Chamberlain?" Ruger asked.

Sarah stared out the window, her arms drawn over her chest as she felt her two worlds closing in, clashing, battling to see which was the strongest. "I don't think so. But Detective Jefferson . . . he seems sharp."

"I agree. He was very inquisitive and seemed to sense there was more to this than a regular break-in."

She glanced at him. "You heard they found Clayton's car and there was blood inside. Maybe this is connected. Maybe that guy in Dorothy's house is responsible."

"It's definitely a possibility."

"What are we going to do?" Her voice trembled slightly.

His jaw twitched as he stared straight ahead. "I think it's time for you to get out of town. As soon as we get back to your place, I'm going to call Charlie and see if she can send a plane or if she wants us to drive. I don't know yet. But you're not safe here."

"What if I don't want to leave?"

Ruger did a double take at her, almost as if her words had startled him. "What do you mean?"

What *did* she mean? Sarah rummaged through her thoughts until she realized she was overthinking this. She knew *exactly* what she meant. She simply had to be brave enough to say it.

"I'm tired of running." As her voice cracked, she rubbed her throat.

"So, what are you suggesting?" Ruger sounded cautious—almost apprehensive.

Sarah stared out the window again, thoughts swirling inside her head—thoughts she desperately wanted to make sense of. "What would it take to put Bryce behind bars? What if I went forward to the police now about what happened? Now that I feel stronger, maybe I can tell them what he did to me. Maybe . . . I don't know. Maybe something can change."

Ruger's jaw twitched again before he finally said, "The police need proof, evidence. Maybe even some video footage or some marks on your skin or witnesses to prove what he did to you. I don't say that to be discouraging. But it's reality in these situations."

Sarah felt herself deflating at his words. "When I married Bryce, he slowly stripped away my identity. Basically, I lost . . . who I was. Then when I left him, I had to leave behind all the people I cared about. I haven't seen my nieces or nephews in two years. Two. Years."

"I can imagine how hard that must be."

"Just now, I've finally started to rebuild. To remember who I really am. To make a new life for myself. I don't want to start all over again. Part of me would rather . . ."

He threw her a sharp glance.

"Don't get me wrong. I don't want to die," she quickly corrected. "I'm not suicidal, if that's what it sounds like. But I feel myself growing weary. I have to wonder if this is all worth it."

"Sarah . . ." He reached over and squeezed her

hand. "*You're* worth it. Never forget that."

She pressed her eyes shut and let his words wash over her.

Those were the words she needed to hear at this very moment.

She would not be defined by the lies Bryce had drilled into her.

Her life *was* worth fighting for.

"I guess that's what I'm trying to say." Sarah shrugged. "Part of me would rather . . . fight for the life I want than to live in constant fear."

———

Ruger knew that whatever he did he could *not* put Sarah's life in danger.

What exactly did she have in mind?

He was about to ask her as he slowly headed down the road toward her house. But as soon as he pulled close to the house, his headlights illuminated a broken window on the front. Illuminated the open front door.

Sarah gasped. "No . . ."

Ruger's jaw tightened as he realized it wasn't safe here.

Why hadn't his security system alerted him?

Unless someone had taken it offline. It wasn't likely, but it *was* possible. In fact, what if that was how someone had been bypassing the system all along? Without internet, the system didn't operate. If someone was smart enough, they could manipulate service at Sarah's house—maybe even do that remotely.

In other circumstances, Ruger might hop out of the SUV to check things out himself. But given the dire situation Sarah was in, he couldn't risk that. Besides, whoever did this was probably long gone. They'd probably only wanted to send a message.

Ruger didn't say the words aloud, but he was nearly certain Bryce had been here. Charlie had said he mentioned he was supposed to come out west on vacation.

Montana was definitely out west.

As he turned the vehicle around, Sarah remained quiet beside him. Ruger knew she was probably lost in thought, which was understandable considering everything that had happened.

He didn't push her to talk. She needed the space to sort through everything.

Several minutes later, he pulled up to one of the more popular motels in town—a place with rooms accessible directly from the outside. They needed the safety of being in a more public space right now that would provide easy access to his SUV.

"Stay here," he muttered to Sarah. "And lock the door behind me."

He parked where he'd be able to see his vehicle from inside the lobby.

Thankfully, tourist season in this area was mostly over, so the place had vacancies. He rented a room on the first floor.

Then he drove across the parking lot and parked directly in front of his room. With one last glance around, Ruger ushered Sarah inside.

As soon as they were in the room, he locked the door behind them and peered outside again to make sure no one was watching. He'd been careful on the way here, and he hadn't seen anybody following.

But he still needed to be on guard.

Finally, he turned to Sarah. When he saw the apprehension etched into the tight lines of her face, he wanted nothing more than to soothe her fears somehow.

So, when Sarah fell into his arms, he didn't argue. Instead, he held her, all too aware of the way her heart pounded against his chest.

He stroked her hair and whispered soothing words.

But that was all.

He'd meant it when he said he needed to keep his distance.

No more kisses.

He couldn't even allow himself to be tempted because, if he did, he wasn't sure he'd be able to resist.

When Sarah pulled away, he studied her face. Studied the moisture in her gaze. The lines around her eyes. The way her lips trembled.

His throat tightened at the sight of her fear. "Are you okay?"

"Not really."

He'd known that was the truth. Nothing he could do would make this situation okay.

But he would keep trying.

He stepped back, still struggling with his desire to hold her. "For now, let's get some sleep and, in the morning, we'll figure this out. Okay?"

Sarah seemed almost reluctant as she nodded. "Okay."

Ruger prayed tomorrow would be a better day— one where they finally discovered some answers.

But before he went to bed, he had one more thing to do. He needed to call Charlie.

She needed to send backup.

He knew his colleagues were still working several

big cases and that the organization was stretched thin right now.

But he needed at least one other guy here to watch his back, especially as danger closed in.

THIRTY-FOUR

AS MUCH AS Sarah wanted to sleep, she couldn't. Instead, she tossed and turned in bed nearly all night.

She knew it was the same for Ruger. He didn't toss and turn, though. Instead, he stared at the ceiling. She could see the dim glow from the bathroom light catching his eyes.

Too much was going on for either of them to get any sleep.

But neither said anything nor acknowledged the other.

It was better that way. Better if they kept their distance. *Especially* since they were alone in this motel room.

Sarah hadn't had a chance to grab anything from her place—she'd known it wouldn't be safe to go inside. She shuddered every time she thought about her broken window. Her open front door.

Maybe—*maybe*—she and Ruger would go back to her place in the daylight.

The person doing this was becoming more brazen, she realized. He didn't want to hide his presence. He wanted to make it clear and evident instead.

That thought didn't bring Sarah any comfort.

As soon as the sun began to rise, she quietly slid out of bed and into the shower. Standing under the spray of warm water usually helped to clarify her thoughts.

She had been scheduled to work, but her boss had told her while at Dorothy's place to take a couple of days off. Sarah had agreed that was the best decision. She didn't want to put any of her patients in danger.

Once finished in the shower, she dried off and got dressed in her scrubs from yesterday. Since she wasn't going into work, she didn't bother to dry her hair.

When she stepped out of the bathroom, Ruger was already up and peering out the window. He dropped the curtain when he saw her.

"I fixed a pot of coffee." He nodded to a pot on the counter. "It's not very good, but if you need some —like I do—it's there."

Sarah poured some into a Styrofoam cup,

frowning as she took a sip and the bitterness washed over her tastebuds. Despite the taste, she muttered, "Thank you."

She took another glance at Ruger, wondering what he was thinking. He already seemed pensive, as if his sleepless night had only clarified the danger of this situation.

"Is it too early to talk about our plans for today?" She lowered herself on the edge of the bed. "To decide what we're going to do?"

He let out a deep breath, almost as if he were burdened. Sarah hated to put him in this position. Yet she knew without him by her side, she wouldn't survive. It wasn't something she wanted to admit. She wanted to be strong.

But, if she was being realistic, she'd admit her limitations.

"Charlie is sending two guys here. They're wrapping up something else right now, so they can't be here until the afternoon. In the meantime, she told us to stay put."

"That seems like a good idea. Are they coming to take us to Arizona? Or . . ."

Ruger's jaw flexed. "That's what we need to figure out before they get here. The decision is up to you."

Before Ruger could say anything else, a knock sounded at the door.

"Police!"

Ruger and Sarah exchanged glances.

He then turned, glanced out the peephole, and stepped back. "It really is the police."

Panic shot through Sarah as her thoughts raced. "What are they doing here? Do you think they have an update?"

"They don't usually send four squad cars if they have an update." His jaw visibly tightened.

Sarah's lungs froze at his words. "Four squad cars? Why in the world would they do that?"

"I have a feeling we're about to find out."

The knock came again, faster and louder this time.

"I don't know what's about to happen." Ruger locked gazes with her as if trying to silently communicate. "But I've got to answer this door."

Slowly—almost reluctantly—he took the chain lock off and twisted the lock. Before he could turn the knob, Detective Jefferson barged inside.

His intense gaze paused on Ruger. "Ruger Stark, we need to bring you in for questioning."

"Questioning? About what?"

"The death of Clayton Barney."

Ruger's thoughts raced as Detective Jefferson took his arm. "I don't know what you think, but I didn't kill anyone."

"We'll see about that." Without explaining anything else, the detective led him toward one of the squad cars.

"I have a concealed carry permit, and a gun tucked into my waistband," he told Jefferson, knowing he needed to be upfront.

One of the officers took the gun from him before patting him down for more weapons.

As he did, Ruger glanced back at Sarah. Her lips parted with surprise. Lines of worry stretched across her forehead. Concern filled her eyes.

Just as he was about to tell her to stay in the room, another officer gripped her arm. "We need to take you in for questioning again also."

Ruger didn't know if that made him feel better or worse. At least, Sarah would be with the police, which might mean she was safer.

But nothing seemed certain right now.

What evidence did the cops think they had to bring him in? Thankfully, he wasn't being arrested —not yet.

At the station in the interrogation room, Ruger sat alone for at least an hour.

Finally, Detective Jefferson came back into the room and explained why Ruger had been brought in.

"Clayton Barney's body was discovered in the woods on the outskirts of town this morning." The detective stood against the wall with his arms crossed. "He was stabbed multiple times."

Ruger observed the detective carefully, knowing that one wrong move or word could land him in jail. "I'm sorry to hear that. But just because his body was found, why does that make me a suspect?"

"We got an anonymous tip leading us to you."

"So, you assume I'm guilty?"

"I don't make assumptions. I look at the facts. And evidence. After we brought you in this morning, we searched your vehicle, and we found a bloody knife under the seat in your SUV. We're running it through the system now and testing the blood, but we're betting it's a match."

Shock coursed through Ruger.

The knife was in his vehicle? That wasn't possible.

If someone had gotten into his SUV, he would have heard the car alarm.

Unless they'd circumvented the alarm and quietly gotten inside while he was sleeping.

"Someone planted it there." Ruger locked his gaze with the detective's.

Jefferson grunted as if unconvinced.

"How did you even know where I was staying?" Ruger asked.

"It's a small town. It wasn't hard to figure out. We also know about your argument with Mr. Barney at the pharmacy. His wife confirmed that you went to their house as well."

Ruger couldn't believe this. Had he been set up?

It was the only thing that made sense.

Someone wanted to separate him from Sarah.

And the only person Ruger could think of who'd want to do that was Bryce.

Alarm rushed through him.

Ruger needed to protect her. But he wouldn't be able to do that from the confines of the police station.

Still, there had to be *something* he could do.

He stared at the detective.

Should he tell this man the truth?

Ruger didn't want to. He didn't want to break Sarah's cover. If he did, would Sarah even be able to live here in this town anymore? Or would she have to start again?

He weighed his options carefully, knowing Sarah's future depended on what he said next.

"HAVE you been having any recent issues you want to tell us about?" Detective Jefferson stared at Sarah from across the interrogation table at the police station.

Sarah blinked in surprise at his question. "Recent issues? Like what?"

The only person she could think of who might have mentioned any issues to the police was Pierce. But, even then, he seemed to think that Ruger wasn't treating her well. Pierce never mentioned mental health problems—if that's what he meant by "recent issues."

No, that sounded more like something Bryce would do.

Chills suddenly rushed up her spine.

The detective had been in the room with her for

five minutes—long enough to explain that Clayton's body had been found on the outskirts of town and that an anonymous tip had led the cops to Ruger.

"Tell us about the argument Mr. Stark had with Clayton Barney." The detective leaned back and crossed one leg over the other as he patiently waited for her answer.

Sarah's mind raced as she considered how much she should say. The truth would be the simplest. But would she dig herself into a hole if she told him about her past?

She only had a moment to decide.

She swallowed hard, deciding to dip her toe in the water. She wouldn't tell him everything—but she'd tell him some.

"I take medication for my thyroid," she started. "But after I got my last prescription refill, I noticed I felt differently. That's when I sent some of those pills off to be tested. It turned out the meds I was given weren't my thyroid medications at all. They were opioids laced with fentanyl."

There it was. Sarah had laid it out.

That revelation certainly couldn't lead back to the fact that her name really wasn't Sarah Chamberlain.

Could it?

However, if telling the truth was what she had to do in order to prove that Ruger was innocent, then that's what she'd do. Sarah wasn't going to let Ruger take the fall for this.

The detective narrowed his eyes. "How did you have the medication tested?"

She hoped her story didn't sound flimsy. The average person probably didn't have the same resources at hand that Charlie Soldier did. Certainly, the detective would realize that.

"I know a guy who does it," she finally offered. "I was desperate and asked him for his help."

Detective Jefferson narrowed his eyes even more. "So, you thought Clayton was responsible?"

"He works at the pharmacy where I pick up my meds, so I wanted to ask him some questions. He said he'd meet us after work, but he never showed. That's when Ruger and I went to his house to see if everything was okay. But his wife said he hadn't come home."

The detective shifted in his seat. "Why would Clayton replace your meds?"

Sarah shrugged. "That's what I was trying to figure out—if it was an accident or not."

The detective studied her carefully, and Sarah knew the next part of this conversation would be pivotal.

"Did you ever think about reporting this to the police?" he asked. "That's a pretty serious offense."

"I did think about it. But I wanted to talk to Clayton first, give him a chance to explain. Unfortunately, that opportunity never came. We never saw him again after that."

"Are you sure?"

"Of course, I'm sure." She paused. "You think Ruger killed him, don't you?"

Detective Jefferson didn't deny her words.

She rubbed her hands together as her thoughts continued to race. "And you should know that my house appeared to have been broken into earlier. A window was smashed, and the front door was open."

"Was anything stolen?"

"We didn't go inside. It didn't seem safe."

"And you didn't report that either?" Skepticism stretched through his voice.

"I . . . I just needed to gather my thoughts first. I don't like drawing attention to myself. I know it sounds strange but . . . I'm just a very private person."

The detective let out a soft grunt. "You said you and Mr. Stark go way back? To Houston?"

Sarah's throat tightened as she wondered what he was getting at. Was he suspicious about their connection? Had he put together the fact that Sarah didn't have a real past until she came here to Kalispell?

"That's correct." Her throat burned as she said the words.

"Are the two of you romantically involved?"

She shook her head, pushing aside thoughts of their kiss. Of Ruger's hesitation. Of his integrity. "No, we're not."

"And yet you spent the night together in the motel room. Just the two of you?"

"It's not what you think."

Detective Jefferson nodded slowly again.

Sarah knew exactly what he was thinking, and she didn't like where he was going with this.

Her future hinged on the rest of this conversation. She could feel it in her bones.

Ruger tried to convince Detective Jefferson to let him talk to Sarah, but the man refused.

The detective had been bouncing back and forth between the two of them.

Now he was back with Ruger again.

"Tell me about your relationship with Ms. Chamberlain." This time the detective sat in front of him, his demeanor remaining even-keeled and unemotional. "She's a beautiful woman. Certainly, a single guy like you is attracted to her."

Ruger stared at him and shrugged, realizing the man was just trying to get into his head. "It's like I said, we're old friends."

"Would you say you two are . . . close?"

"I care about her. Is that what you want to know?"

"Did you want to teach Clayton Barney a lesson for messing with her medications?"

Ruger shook his head. "No, not at all. I just wanted to have a conversation with him. Innocent until proven guilty, right? I hope that's true for me as well."

"It sounds like that conversation got pretty heated. Several people witnessed it at the pharmacy."

"It wasn't heated." Ruger also remained calm, knowing any emotion would be held against him. "But I was very firm with Clayton when I told him we needed to talk. As soon as I brought the subject up, the man got cagey. Let's face the facts here. If he was messing with Sarah's medications, then maybe he was messing with other people's medications as well. That would give people plenty of reasons to be angry with him."

"That might be true." Detective Jefferson pulled a pen from his pocket and tapped it against the table, seemingly in tempo with his thoughts. "But what we're lacking here is motive. *Why?* Why would Mr. Barney go through all that trouble?"

Ruger shrugged, feeling like the detective was simply playing some kind of mind game with him. "That's something that you'll have to figure out yourself. But maybe Clayton was getting some type of payout for it. He and his family have a nice house, and he just bought an expensive new car for his wife. Look at his financials and maybe they'll tell you something."

The detective grunted. "You're former Secret Service, so your line of reasoning doesn't surprise me. We've already looked into Mr. Barney's financial records, and he did receive a large payout."

Ruger's pulse ticked faster. "Then maybe you can trace that back to the person who sent it to him."

"We tried. It was a cash deposit."

Ruger bit back a frown. "Of course, it was."

He'd already guessed as much. But he needed to get to the bottom of this, and he wasn't going to find any answers sitting in this room.

The more time he spent away from Sarah, the more danger she could be in.

Charlie could help. But unfortunately, since he hadn't been formally arrested, he wasn't entitled to a phone call.

He needed to try one more time to see if he could get a message to Sarah.

He leaned on the table toward the detective. "Please, I need to talk to Sarah."

Detective Jefferson stared at him, a hard look in his gaze. "I'm sorry. But that's not going to happen."

CHAPTER
THIRTY-SIX

THREE HOURS after arriving at the station, the police let Sarah go.

She asked to talk to Ruger, but Detective Jefferson told her that it wasn't a possibility.

As she stood in the police station lobby, a feeling of helplessness washed over her. The police had offered to give her a ride back to the motel, but she refused.

She wanted to get away from them. They didn't feel safe right now—not since they'd detained Ruger.

She hadn't told the detective everything. Hadn't told him about her past life.

Now she wondered if that was a mistake.

But it wasn't too late. She could still turn around and tell them everything.

First, she just needed to be certain that was the right thing to do.

The truth was, she could be arrested on the spot for identity fraud once she made that admission. What she'd done when she started over wasn't government sanctioned like witness protection was.

She wasn't sure what exactly would be solved by her admission.

She couldn't get Ruger out of jail if she was also behind bars.

But she did know who *could* help. Ruger's team members should be arriving at the motel soon.

She'd let them know what was happening, and they could all figure out how to handle this.

Sarah glanced out the set of glass doors forming the police station exit. The motel was probably a mile away.

She could walk. Maybe it would be good to clear her head.

Pulling her sweatshirt closer, she stepped out the door, giving one last glance behind her. Ruger was behind one of these walls somewhere.

She frowned.

She'd do whatever she needed to get him out of there.

As she stepped outside and around the corner, she nearly collided with someone.

She drew back, worst-case scenarios racing through her mind.

Then the man's face came into view, and she gasped.

Pierce.

What was he doing here?

Ruger leaned back in his chair in the interrogation room.

Detective Jefferson had disappeared again, leaving Ruger alone with his thoughts.

He needed to call Charlie. She needed to know what was going on. Mateo and Jesse were on their way but, as of right now, Sarah was out there alone.

He clenched his jaw. He should have taken her away from here as soon as they'd found out about the switched medications. Should've brought her to Vanishing Ranch.

But he'd understood Sarah's hesitations for not wanting to go.

Doing so would mean starting over again in a new place with a new identity. What kind of life was that?

The whole situation reminded him of the Bible verse about why the righteous suffered while the wicked prospered. This situation seemed to be the very definition of that.

Ruger waited, the seconds ticking by.

The man who had been in Dorothy's house yesterday obviously wasn't talking. Plus, there didn't seem to be anything to tie him with Clayton.

That left Ruger as the police's number one suspect.

He sighed.

He hated feeling helpless. Hated not knowing where Sarah was. What she was doing. What she was going through.

Certainly, the police couldn't keep him on these charges. They had to see that he was innocent.

That somebody had purposefully planted that knife in his SUV.

Ruger contemplated his options.

Maybe he wouldn't tell Sarah's whole story.

But unless he told part of it, there was a good chance Sarah wouldn't survive this ordeal.

Once she was safe, they could worry about other details.

For now, he had to let Detective Jefferson know Sarah was in danger.

He had no other choice.

But he prayed she would live long enough to forgive him for doing so.

SARAH STEPPED AWAY from Pierce as fear shot through her.

"What are you doing here?" Her voice trembled as she asked the question.

He stepped closer, his expression tight with worry. "I heard what happened, and I wanted to check on you."

She pushed a hair behind her ear, her thoughts racing. "Wait . . . you . . . you heard what happened?"

He shrugged. "It's a small town, and word travels fast. But you already know that." He lowered his voice. "I knew that guy with you was bad news. I'm glad he's behind bars."

She stared at Pierce a moment, trying to read his expression. Was he truly just worried? Or was he behind this? Had he set Ruger up?

She mentally shook her head.

No, that didn't make sense. If that were true, it would mean that Pierce killed Clayton. And what reason would Pierce have for killing Clayton?

As she stared up at Pierce's intense eyes, she was instinctively aware that Pierce knew more than he was letting on.

The one thing certain in her mind right now was that Pierce wasn't a safe person.

Sarah needed to get away from him.

She swallowed hard, straightened her shoulders, and glanced behind him at the sidewalk leading toward her motel. "I'm sorry, but I really can't talk right now."

He moved in front of her as she took a step. "Where are you going? Let me give you a ride."

She shrugged him off, trying to remain calm and not show her fear. "No, that's okay. I need to clear my head."

"But after everything that's happened . . ." His voice softened as if he were empathetic.

She tried to choose her words, her argument. "If Ruger really did kill Clayton, I should be safe now, right?"

It pained her to say those words, but she was desperate to get away. And, if Pierce really believed

Ruger was dangerous, then he shouldn't be able to argue with her.

Something fluttered in his gaze before he nodded. "I guess that makes sense. I just hate for you to be alone at a time like this."

"Being alone is exactly what I need right now." She gave him one last glance before edging past him. "Bye, Pierce."

Before he could say anything else, Sarah hurried down the sidewalk.

But she'd never felt so on edge.

Sarah watched her surroundings during the entire walk to the motel. Every time a car passed or someone else appeared on the sidewalk, she jumped.

Did other people here in town know about what had happened also? Just like Pierce did?

Sarah hardly cared what people thought of her.

She was more concerned that Bryce was here and that these rumors might lead him to her.

What if he was watching her right now?

She continued to glance around, but she didn't see him.

Still, she would remain on guard.

Finally, she reached the motel. Ruger had given her a key last night, and she'd slipped it into her pocket this morning—thankfully. The lady at the front desk probably wouldn't give her one otherwise because Sarah was certain Ruger hadn't given her name when he checked in.

She stepped into the room and quickly locked the door.

Then she looked around.

The police had clearly gone through it. Drawers were open, sheets rumpled, furniture moved.

Sarah sat on the edge of the bed and pulled out the burner phone she'd kept hidden in her purse.

With trembling hands, Sarah dialed Charlie's number, knowing she'd need to know what had happened.

Charlie answered on the first ring. "Is everything okay?"

Sarah told her everything.

"Just stay where you are." Charlie's voice hardened with concern and determination. "I have two guys on their way, Mateo and Jesse. They should be there within two hours. So, hold tight. And thanks for letting me know about Ruger. I'm going to get him out of there if it's the last thing I do."

Sarah swallowed hard. She hoped Charlie was right.

But she instinctively knew they didn't have much time.

CHAPTER
THIRTY-EIGHT

SARAH SAT on the floor near the door of the motel room with her knees pulled to her chest.

No spot in the room seemed safe, but at least here she was away from the windows and out of sight.

Her heart continued to thrum in her ears as she waited for backup to arrive. As she anticipated what trouble might show up.

She gripped the burner phone in her hands.

Thirty minutes had passed since she talked to Charlie. She knew help would be here soon.

The question was, would they arrive soon enough?

She had to think of a way to get Ruger out of jail and clear his name.

She thought about that area of town that Clayton's body was found.

It was close to where Mary lived.

Her thoughts raced.

Mary had a security system that included cameras on the outside of her house.

Had one of those cameras picked up something?

It seemed like a good possibility, something worth checking out.

Sarah could simply tell the police and let them look. But first, she needed to know if her theory was viable. There were too many uncertainties right now. She couldn't be sure who to trust.

She stood, apprehension dashing through her.

How would she get to Mary's? She could walk. The police had taken Ruger's SUV, and her own car was back at her house, which was definitely too far away to walk. She supposed she could call a rideshare service, but she didn't trust being in the car with a stranger right now.

Her mind made up, she pulled up the hood of her sweatshirt, jammed her burner phone into her pocket, and stepped out of the motel room.

She glanced back and forth, again looking for signs of anyone suspicious.

But she saw no one.

Quickly, she closed the motel door behind her and hurried down the street toward Mary's.

She was taking a risk.

But she hoped that this gamble paid off.

Twenty minutes later, Sarah knocked at Mary's door.

The woman answered a few moments later with a bright smile. "Sarah . . . I wasn't expecting to see you today." Her gaze scanned Sarah, and she frowned. "You seem out of sorts."

"Can I come in?" Sarah glanced behind her again but saw no one.

"Of course, of course." Mary opened the door wider, and Sarah slipped inside. She was certain to lock the door, just to be safe.

Replays of the incident yesterday at Dorothy's house pummeled her thoughts.

Mary had practically become like a grandmother to her. The last thing she wanted was to do anything to put this woman in danger. To put *any* of her patients in danger.

She prayed she didn't regret this move.

She hadn't seen anyone watching her, but that didn't mean they weren't.

"What can I do for you?" Mary looked up at her, a sweet expression on her face as she patiently waited for Sarah to explain why she was here.

"I'm sure you've heard about everything that's

happened here in town," Sarah started, feeling another rumble of nerves.

Mary nodded, but her eyes contained no judgment. "I did hear a few things. Rumors. I don't believe any of them. And, of course, I don't believe that hubba hubba hunk of a man is guilty of anything."

Sarah felt a strange relief at her words. "He's innocent, and I'm trying to prove it."

"So, you came here?" Her eyebrows climbed with curiosity.

"I know this may sound like a strange request, but I was wondering if I could see the footage from your security cameras."

Mary blinked as if the proposition surprised her. Then, she snapped out of her surprise and nodded. "If you would like to, then, of course."

Sarah followed Mary through the house to an old desktop computer in a spare bedroom.

As she sat at the desk, she turned to Mary. "Did you hear the commotion this morning when the police discovered the body?"

Mary rubbed her hands together, almost as if Sarah's questions were making her anxious. "I did. Is that what this is about? Do you think my cameras picked up something?"

"I'm kind of surprised the police haven't come here to ask you questions themselves."

"Now that you mention it, I am too. Maybe they haven't thought about it yet. Things like this don't happen very often here in Kalispell. They're more equipped to deal with robberies or breaking up brawls."

Or maybe they'd just decided that Ruger was guilty, and they were no longer looking for any more evidence . . . Sarah kept that thought to herself.

"How far back do you want to scroll?" Mary leaned toward the keyboard. "I'm not sure how to use this exactly, but I'm sure we can figure it out."

"If you don't mind, first I'd like to see the footage from when the police discovered the body," Sarah said.

After a few tries, the two of them managed to find the footage. Sarah watched as police cars pulled onto the scene and officers tramped toward the woods.

Thirty minutes later, even more police cars surrounded the area and the whole road was blocked off.

Now, Sarah needed to scroll back further and figure out if she could pinpoint the time Clayton's body had been left there . . . and by whom.

CHAPTER
THIRTY-NINE

FINALLY, Detective Jefferson came back into the interrogation room to talk to Ruger. He brought him a bottle of water and set it on the table in front of him.

"Am I still being held?" Ruger asked.

"That murder weapon being left in your car is hard to ignore." Detective Jefferson rolled his head to the side and rubbed his neck—the first sign he'd shown of exhaustion.

Ruger shook his head. "I'm a former cop and former Secret Service. Do you think I'd really be dumb enough to leave the murder weapon in my vehicle if I was the one who did this? Do you really think I would even stay in town? Or that I'd murder someone with a knife? There are much more efficient ways of doing things."

The detective twisted his head. "I can't deny anything you just said."

Ruger gave him a smoldering stare.

He was still worried about Sarah. Were they still holding her here? If not, where had she gone?

But the biggest question in his mind was: was she okay?

"You can't deny anything I said, yet you're still detaining me," Ruger finally said.

"We're trying to be thorough."

Ruger leaned forward. "Let me ask you this . . . you said you got an anonymous tip that that knife was in my SUV. Do you have any idea who gave you that tip?"

Detective Jefferson shrugged. "I don't."

"Was it a phone call? An email? Is there a way to trace it?"

The detective remained silent a moment before finally letting out a long sigh. "A note was left under my windshield this morning, if you must know."

"Here or at home?"

"Here."

"You do have security cameras outside the station here, don't you? Can't you see who left it?"

The detective's gaze darkened as if he didn't appreciate the tables being turned. "We looked. The person was wearing black and a hat. His face was concealed."

"Isn't that suspicious within itself? If someone had this tip, why not just come forward? Why go through all the cloak-and-dagger tactics to get this information to you?"

"Another good question, but there are numerous reasons why people like to remain anonymous."

Ruger leaned back and crossed his arms, still not touching his water. "Maybe it's because someone set me up."

"Who would do that?"

"I have no idea."

"I don't think you're telling the truth."

The detective had a point. Ruger swallowed hard as he contemplated his words.

Could he trust this man?

That was the question of the hour.

In order to make any progress, Ruger was going to need to share some of what had happened.

But he would have to choose his words carefully.

"Sarah's life is in danger," Ruger finally said.

His words seemed to get the detective's attention, and Jefferson straightened. "What do you mean?"

"I mean, she was married before to a vile man who'd like nothing more than to make her pay for leaving him. Right now, Sarah is out there alone. And

I have a feeling her ex-husband was the one behind this."

Sarah paused the video at the 1:31 a.m. mark and watched.

A dark-colored sedan pulled up to the side of the curb.

There had been no other movement on the street until then. Not for the previous fifteen minutes. Most people in this area were in bed long before then, resting up for their next big adventure.

A figure dressed in black got out and opened the trunk. He lifted something from the back.

Something that looked an awful lot like a body.

Sarah's heart beat harder.

Part of her wished Mary wasn't here to watch this. She wasn't sure the woman could handle the trauma, considering her health condition.

But Mary had made it clear she wasn't going anywhere. She claimed she watched enough *Dateline* specials to be able to handle this.

The man carried the body from his car into the woods. When he returned, his hands were empty.

This was it, Sarah realized. This was the killer.

He'd disposed of Clayton's body, and then he'd driven away.

Unfortunately, it was too dark outside to read the license plate. Sarah definitely couldn't make out any of the man's features.

But it wasn't Ruger. It wasn't his car. Besides, Ruger was with her last night in that motel room.

Would that be enough to convince the police?

It was worth a shot.

Sarah turned to Mary. "Can I make a copy of this?"

"Sure. I don't know how, but if you can figure it out."

Mary didn't have a jump drive or a CD or anything to burn a copy onto.

Instead, Sarah took a video of the footage using her cell phone. She'd show the police this, and, if they had any integrity, they would come here to get a copy of this themselves.

Sarah glanced at Mary one more time.

Did the killer have any idea that this sweet woman might have his image on camera? If he did, she'd be a target also.

That was even more reason why Sarah needed to get to the police station and show them this herself. A phone call wouldn't do.

Sarah sucked on her lip a moment before saying,

"I hate to ask you this, but is there any chance I can use your car?"

"My car?" Mary shrugged. "I haven't started it in a while."

"That's okay. I need to take this footage to the police. I'm going to ask them to send an officer out here to stay with you."

Mary's eyes widened. "To stay with me?"

She squeezed the woman's bony hand. "Just to be on the safe side. They're going to want a copy of this video for themselves too, something more than what I just recorded with my phone."

"Whatever you need. That'll be fine with me. I'm a tough old broad."

"But I *am* concerned about you." Sarah frowned as she wondered what to do.

"If it makes you feel better, I'll keep my doors locked and only use my intercom."

"That would make me feel better."

Mary nodded. "Then that's what I'll do."

AFTER SARAH WAS sure that Mary was secure in her home, she took the car keys and hurried outside.

It was well past lunchtime by now.

She hadn't heard from Charlie, but backup should be here at any minute.

Still, Sarah didn't have any time to waste.

She had to get to the police station. With any luck, once they watched this video Ruger would be released.

She clutched the car keys that Mary had given her. Then she hurried to the car, glancing around one more time.

She still didn't see anyone watching or lurking.

Part of her felt relieved at the thought. She didn't

want someone to follow her. But another part felt suspicious, almost like this was too easy.

If someone had gone through the trouble of planting evidence to indicate Ruger, this person probably had other tricks up his sleeve also.

Maybe this person wasn't planning to act now. Maybe he wasn't planning something for the daylight hours.

But Sarah would worry about that later.

For now, she climbed into the car and cranked the engine.

The car started.

Relief rushed through her.

But just as she put the car into Reverse, a noise stirred behind her.

When she looked into the rearview mirror, a familiar face stared at her from the back seat.

***

Detective Jefferson stepped back into the interrogation room again. This time, his expression was no longer accusatory.

"You're free to go. I'll have one of my guys bring you your gun."

Ruger straightened, uncertain if he'd heard correctly. "I am?"

The detective seemed to nod almost begrudgingly. "That's right. We checked the security footage at the motel. It took some time to get the owner to cooperate. That said, we know you didn't leave your room all night."

Ruger waited, sensing the man had something else to say.

Jefferson pressed his lips together a moment before continuing, "A figure in black was seen walking toward your SUV. The camera was on the wrong side to pick up exactly what he was doing, we now believe that he was planting the evidence in your SUV, just as you said."

Ruger sucked in a quick breath, outrage rushing through him—outrage that he contained. "Do you have any idea who it was?"

Detective Jefferson shook his head. "Unfortunately, we are unable to make out any details. But we're trying to check the security camera footage from the surrounding areas to see if we can figure out who this is. We appreciate your cooperation. We're sorry to have troubled you."

Troubled him? That seemed like an understatement.

But Ruger didn't say that.

Instead, he said, "I need a ride to the motel to check on Sarah."

"We sent an officer to sit outside the motel room about twenty minutes ago, and she hasn't left since he arrived."

That made Ruger feel a little better, but not much. "I'd still like a ride."

"Of course. And if you discover anything that will help us to pinpoint who did this to Clayton, I'd appreciate knowing."

"Will do." Although, Ruger didn't feel like Detective Jefferson was exactly his friend right now.

A few minutes later, when Ruger walked inside the motel room he'd rented, the place was empty.

He strode toward the officer stationed outside in his cruiser. The officer rolled the window down and stared up at him. "Everything okay?"

"She's not in there."

The officer blinked in surprise. "No one has left that room."

Ruger's shoulders tightened even more. "How long was Sarah here before you got here?"

"I don't know." He shrugged. "I was just told to station myself here and make sure there was no trouble inside."

Ruger didn't like the sound of that. How long had she been gone already?

He tried her phone, but there was no answer.

Instead, he leaned toward the officer again.

"What are the odds the owner of this place will let you see any security footage? I need to know if she left here on her own free will or not."

This guy would have better chances of finding that information than Ruger.

The officer climbed from his car. "I'll see what I can do."

While he did that, Ruger went through a mental timeline.

He wasn't sure exactly when Sarah had been released. But there was a good possibility that she hadn't even come back to the motel room from the police station, even though that's what he'd instructed her to do.

The woman definitely had a mind of her own.

As worst-case scenarios pummeled him, he realized he needed to figure out what to do, and he needed to figure it out now.

Just as the thought went through his head, two vehicles pulled into the lot.

Two of his team members—Mateo and Jesse—stepped out.

A brief moment of relief washed through Ruger.

Backup was here.

Maybe they could split up and find Sarah.

COLD WASHED through Sarah's body in waves.

"Bryce . . . you found me." Her voice trembled.

His face filled her rearview mirror. His blond hair brushed back neatly. His icy blue eyes. His even features.

He still looked like an upstanding citizen—even with his gun.

His looks were what had made her trust him. He'd seemed like an honorable, all-American man.

He was anything but.

"There's no time to talk here," he barked. "Right now, you need to drive."

He pointed the gun at her.

Sarah knew he wouldn't hesitate to use it.

"I said move," Bryce growled, pressing the gun into the seat.

She could feel the barrel against her back.

Her hands trembled as she put the car into Reverse. She slowly backed out of the driveway and onto the street.

"Head east," he said.

Everything blurred around her. This was all happening too quickly yet in slow motion.

Bryce had found her.

Now he was going to kill her.

By listening to his instructions, she was just prolonging her death.

A shudder raced through her.

Part of her wondered if maybe, instead of enduring whatever he planned for her, she should just let him pull the trigger.

But she feared for too many other people in her life—including Mary.

Even though the woman was locked inside her house, there was still a chance she was in danger.

"Where are we going?" She gripped the wheel, hardly able to breathe as she headed down the road.

"To your place."

To her place? Why would they go there?

What exactly did he have planned?

She wasn't sure. But the more information she had, the easier it would be to make an informed decision.

"How did you find me?" she asked, stealing another glance at him.

"Do you remember Charles Conley?"

Her thoughts raced as she tried to place the name. "He was one of your colleagues at the hospital, right? An anesthesiologist?"

"That's right. He came out here on a hunting trip. Said he thought he saw you. Of course, he brushed it off and just thought it was someone who looked like you. I've always been suspicious and thought there was more to your so-called death than met the eye. I knew when your body never washed up that you didn't actually die."

"I see." Her voice cracked.

"I acted like a grieving husband, of course. But it's always been my goal to find you. And now I have."

She swallowed hard. "Yes, you have."

With his free hand, Bryce reached up and stroked her hair. "I personally like you as a blonde better. But the new look is intriguing."

Disgust roiled in her stomach. The last thing she wanted was Bryce's approval.

"You didn't think that you were really going to be able to get away, did you?" His breath brushed her ear. "You're mine. You've always been mine."

She kept her eyes on the road. But his possessive

words made her body and mind want to freeze. To panic. To quake.

She kept breathing, trying to stay focused. "You're remarried. You have a new wife."

Sarah often wondered how he treated her. Marsha.

She knew she shouldn't have, but once she'd gone to the library and looked Bryce up. Seen the pictures of his wedding.

But she knew what most likely lurked beneath the photo of their smiling faces.

Toxicity.

If Bryce's track record held steady, the new Mrs. Daniels was in a bad place also.

"Marsha is nothing like you," he crooned. "She obeys me."

Sarah heard the coldness in his tone and shuddered.

"You're my one and only. Remember how I always told you that?"

He did always tell her that, usually after his fist collided with her abdomen or his palm smashed into her cheek.

"What are you going to do with me?" She glanced in the rearview mirror at him, but as she did, the car drifted to the side of the road. She quickly jerked it back into her lane.

"Watch what you're doing. A car accident isn't one of the plans I have for you."

Panic rumbled inside her at his words.

What was she going to do? How was this all going to end?

"We need to split up and see if we can find her," Ruger said.

He just spent the last ten minutes catching Jesse and Mateo up. It was ten minutes that they didn't have, but they needed to know what was going on.

"Where else could she be?" Mateo asked.

At his question, the officer knocked at the door and held up his phone. "I just talked to the lady at the reception desk. She showed me the security footage, and it looks like Ms. Chamberlain walked out of here about an hour and a half ago. She headed west toward Main Street."

West on Main Street? Where would she have gone? And why?

"Something isn't adding up." Ruger turned to Jesse. "Sarah knew you were on your way. She knew to wait for you here. I need you to drive by Pierce Denning's house and see if he's there. If Bryce isn't behind this, I have a feeling Pierce is. Mateo and I are going to look for Sarah."

"Will do," Jesse said.

As Ruger and Mateo headed in the direction Sarah had gone, Ruger kept his eyes peeled for any sign of her.

She didn't have her vehicle. So, where would she have walked? Her cabin was too far away. Who in this town would she trust enough to ask for a ride?

As they started past Main Street, Ruger glanced down the road, and his thoughts paused a moment.

"Head that way." He pointed to Mary's place.

He knew Sarah had a special connection with this woman. If there was anyone in this town she trusted, it would be Mary.

A moment later, they pulled up at the woman's house.

As Ruger stepped out of the car, he noticed that Mary's car was gone. Ruger had been here twice since he'd arrived in town, and each time it hadn't looked as if the vehicle had been moved in months.

Maybe he was onto something.

He rang the bell, and a moment later a voice came through a speaker there. "Yes?"

"Ms. Mary? This is Ruger. I'm a friend of—"

"Oh, yes, I recognize you. You're Sarah's friend."

The way the woman said "friend" made it clear she thought there was more to that story.

"Have you seen Sarah?" he asked.

"She was just here. She borrowed my car."

"Do you know where she was going?"

"She said to the police station. She found some footage from my security camera that proved you weren't the one who dumped the body in the woods. She was going to show the recording to the detective."

Ruger's heart pounded harder.

Sarah had never shown up there. Ruger would have known if she did. That cop stationed outside of her motel would've said something.

"You said you had security cameras here?" Ruger leaned closer to the speaker, not wanting anyone walking by to hear his conversation.

"That's right. They cover every angle of the outside of my house."

"Is there any way I can see the videos?"

"Of course. I'll be there in a second."

But Ruger knew he didn't have any time to waste right now. He'd leave Mateo here to scour the videos.

While he did that, Ruger needed to be out on the streets combing them to find out what happened to Sarah.

FORTY-TWO

SARAH'S HEAD was swirling by the time she pulled up to her cabin.

Bryce didn't want her to park in the driveway. Instead, he directed her to drive through the grass, toward the trees in the back where she could pull between some of them and park.

No doubt that was because he didn't want the car to be seen too easily—a smart move on his part.

He directed her from the vehicle and toward the back of her property near the lake, his gun still pointed at her.

"Where are we going?" Sarah stopped at the shoreline.

As she did, Bryce stepped closer, a strange look in his eyes as he observed her.

"I loved you so much," he said, his wispy voice a

mixture of affection and evil. "Why can't you understand that?"

Nausea churned inside her. "When you love
someone, you don't punch them. You don't push
them down the stairs and leave them in pain and
suffering."

"Oh, Sarah . . . anything I did was ultimately for
your good." He ran a finger down the side of her
face. "I was just trying to make you into someone
worthy to be a Daniels."

"You have a strange way of doing things then."
Her trembling voice belied the courage she wanted to
show.

"You should've never left me." His hand drifted
from her face to her bicep, and he squeezed it.

His grip tightened with every word until Sarah
finally yelped.

"Do you know how humiliating it would be for
me if word gets out that you faked your death?" he
demanded.

"I'm sure your reputation would be ruined," she
said through clenched teeth.

"I can't let that happen. You understand, don't
you?"

"What are you planning on doing?" She searched
his cold blue eyes for the answers. Although she
wasn't sure she really wanted to know.

"It would be fitting that since you supposedly died by drowning that you actually do."

A shiver raked through her.

If he forced her into the water . . . she wouldn't survive long. The water was too cold. She was lucky the lake hadn't destroyed her earlier this week.

She needed to buy some time.

"You paid Clayton to switch out my medication, didn't you?"

Bryce grinned as if satisfied with himself. "I did. Do you know that sometimes when you're given drugs like that, they play with your mind? They can even make you act out your biggest fears. I had a great time imagining what it might be doing to you."

Was that why she had been drawn to the lake?

"You always wanted to make it seem like I was crazy." She shook her head, her thoughts suddenly clear. Surprisingly clear. Refreshingly clear. "Maybe that was to deflect your own craziness."

His gaze darkened. The next instant, he slapped her.

Her skin stung, and the breath left her lungs.

"Don't talk to me like that," he growled.

"But you can talk to *me* however you want?" When they'd been married, Sarah would've never said something like that. She would have never talked back.

At this point, what did she have to lose? Bryce planned on killing her either way.

"You set Ruger up, didn't you? You paid Clayton to switch out my meds. Then, when that didn't work, you sent that man to grab me at Dorothy's house. When *that* didn't work, you had to take more drastic measures. You planted the murder weapon in Ruger's SUV."

"I don't like the way that guy looks at you. I've been watching the two of you since I got to town. Doesn't he know you're mine?" The words sounded more like a hiss.

"But I'm not yours. Not anymore."

"Enough talking!" he snapped. "I need you to start walking."

"Walking where?"

"Into the lake."

Sarah's heart pounded harder.

Bryce wouldn't know Charlie had sent men to help now that Ruger was in jail.

If she could just buy more time . . .

But when she looked into Bryce's eyes, she knew that wouldn't be possible.

Her time had just run out.

Ruger continued driving the streets of Kalispell searching for Sarah. He knew it was a longshot that he would see her out here, but he had to do something.

But every street he canvassed led nowhere. He didn't see Sarah or the LTD.

He'd already called Charlie. She'd confirmed that Bryce left yesterday for his vacation. But his family—his new wife and parents—had left six hours before him. Apparently, he'd promised to meet them at Lake Tahoe.

Ruger would bet the man decided to take a detour first.

As he got a phone call, he pulled into a parking lot and answered.

It was Mateo.

"I just watched the security video," he started. "A man got into the back of the LTD about ten minutes after Sarah arrived at Mary's house."

Ruger's gut clenched.

It was just what he feared.

"Could you tell who it was?" Ruger asked.

"He had a mask on. Sorry."

"What direction did the car head?"

"East."

East . . . that was the direction of Sarah's house.

Or it could be a way out of town or to the state park even.

Ruger wasn't sure, but he would head that way.

"Jesse is coming back here to pick me up," Mateo said. "Where should we go?"

"I'm driving out to her house. Meet me there. I'll probably need backup."

"Got it."

As soon as Ruger ended that call, he headed back down the street.

This time, he dialed Detective Jefferson's number.

The police needed to know what was going on.

"WALK," Bryce repeated, nodding toward the lake.

A shiver raked through Sarah as she glanced at the glimmering water.

She knew how this would end.

The lake would be her grave. Just as in St. Louis when she'd faked her death, it was the perfect place to hide her body where it would probably never be found.

When she looked again at the gun in his hands, she knew she had little choice but to obey Bryce.

If only she could buy some more time.

Maybe backup would be here soon.

But . . . she couldn't be sure.

She only knew that hope had not died inside her. Not yet. When it did, death would come quickly.

She raised her hands and stepped forward,

knowing if she didn't comply that she'd receive another slap or punch.

Bryce had shown early in their marriage that violence was the consequence of not listening to him.

Before her feet touched the water, voices sounded in the distance.

She and Bryce both froze.

Could that be backup?

No, there was no way Charlie's guys would be that careless or that they'd sound that jovial.

Bryce craned his neck as he glanced at her, his eyes narrowed with accusation. "Expecting company?"

"No, I'm not."

"You were always a terrible liar." He snorted at her before grabbing her arm. Quickly, he pulled her back toward the car and behind a cluster of trees.

From there, they watched.

Sarah's breath caught when she saw two of the guys who'd been camping near her property walking toward them. However, she didn't think they'd actually seen her or Bryce.

"Maybe we'll run into your girlfriend again," one of them said a little too loudly. "She was a hottie."

Both men laughed.

Were they talking about her? Had they wandered

this way to see if they could spot her? Maybe they'd realized this was her property.

From the looks of it, they'd been drinking again.

She'd heard someone was arrested at the state park, and she'd assumed it had been them. Apparently, it wasn't.

She wasn't sure if their appearance was a good or bad thing.

"Say a word or do anything to draw attention to us, and there will be blood," Bryce muttered.

He hadn't said he'd kill the men, but Sarah knew that one, maybe both, of these guys could die.

Bryce wasn't playing any games. If he decided to pull the trigger on one of these men, he would.

He still gripped her arm with one hand and aimed his gun with the other.

If the campers came any closer, they would lose their lives.

Sarah held her breath as she watched and waited, lifting up desperate prayers that the situation wouldn't turn any worse than it already was.

***

The two campers walked toward her cabin and paused, making other lewd comments about Sarah. Comments that made her blush.

Bryce made a weird sound beside her, a grunting noise that showed he didn't appreciate the way they were talking.

Those guys were going to get themselves killed.

Sarah didn't like them. Didn't respect them.

But she didn't want them to die either.

Her heart pounded, pounded, pounded in her ears, each time a rush of blood followed.

Sarah glanced around, looking for something to use as a weapon.

She spotted a couple of sticks and rocks on the ground.

But the instant she tried to grab one, Bryce would notice.

She could feel his gaze assessing everything around him. She'd learned the hard way that nothing got past him.

Nothing.

She stared at the men headed toward her house, wondering what they would do next. If they wandered toward the woods—toward Sarah and Bryce—this whole situation would turn deadly.

The men shifted. Said something indiscernible to each other.

Then they turned.

Walked toward the lake.

Sarah's heart pounded harder with every step. Bryce stepped closer, his breath still hitting her ears.

She could hardly breathe. Even his scent—minty and strong—made her want to throw up.

Just as she thought the guys might veer toward them, they turned back into the woods instead.

She swallowed her relief.

They were safe.

But that meant it was time now for her to die.

As soon as the two guys disappeared, Bryce jerked Sarah toward the lake. His steps were faster this time as if he realized his opportunity could be coming to a close.

Sarah had no doubt he wanted to finish her off and get out of here without anyone noticing he was ever here. And he'd probably succeed.

That was the way things worked with Bryce. He broke all the rules and did everything wrong and only thought about himself . . . yet he prospered.

Her only comfort was in knowing that God was the ultimate judge and jury. Bryce would have to answer to Him one day.

Bryce didn't give her an option to walk into the lake.

Instead, he dragged her in.

The water quickly covered her ankles, then her

knees, and then her waist. The sudden drops in the lake bottom didn't seem to faze him.

The next thing she knew, she was in up to her chest.

Bryce reached under his shirt and shoved his gun into a shoulder holster.

Then he turned back to her.

"It didn't have to end this way," he muttered through gritted teeth. "But you leave me with no other choice."

He grabbed her hair and shoved her underwater.

FORTY-FOUR

RUGER PULLED up to Sarah's house and cut his engine.

He didn't see any cars out front.

But he still needed to check everything out. It made the most sense that Sarah would come here if she was on her own. But if Bryce was calling the shots—and Ruger believed he was—then where would her ex-husband take her?

Maybe not here.

But he needed to be sure.

He couldn't simply chase the wind and expect to catch it. Right now, this was his best lead.

He quietly closed his car door and crept toward the house.

The front door was still open, just as it had been yesterday.

He crept inside, his back to the wall and his gun raised.

But no one was there.

He stepped onto the back deck and glanced at the lake.

The sunlight hit something in the woods, something he hadn't seen there before.

Mary's LTD.

Adrenaline pumped through him at that realization.

He rushed toward the vehicle, not seeing any signs of anyone there.

Where had Bryce taken Sarah? Had he dragged her into the woods?

Doing so didn't seem to fit his character. He had more sophisticated methods of inflicting pain.

But there was no guessing right now. If the man was desperate, he could have done a lot of things.

As soon as Ruger rounded the corner closer to the lake, he saw two people chest-deep in the water. A petite woman and a tall, broad-shouldered man.

Bryce and Sarah . . .

Just as quickly, Sarah's head disappeared.

That's when he realized that Bryce had pushed Sarah under the water and held her there.

As Bryce jerked Sarah by her hair back to the surface, she gulped in a deep breath.

But before her lungs could fully fill with air, she was plunged back under.

Almost immediately, her lungs burned.

Her body screamed for oxygen.

Stars formed in her eyes.

She forced them open underwater.

The lake was clear enough that she could see.

Could see Bryce's legs and waist.

She tried to kick him, but the water slowed her motions. Softened the impact.

He jerked her back up again, and she gasped.

Her reflexes took over as her body fought to survive.

But just as the previous time, before any oxygen could fully fill her lungs, she was plunged under again.

Her mind swirled, her thoughts muddied.

This was it, wasn't it? The moment she would die.

Maybe Sarah had known all along that water would both be her savior and her death.

No doubt Bryce would make it look like an accident. Or that she'd done this to herself. Or he'd tie something to her leg until she sank beneath the water never to be found.

She didn't know how yet. But he would think of a way to get away with this.

When her life was said and done, would there be anyone left to mourn her?

Maybe Ruger. But their relationship had only begun to grow. He hadn't known her long enough to truly mourn.

Maybe some of her patients would miss her. Mary's face filled her mind.

Sarah's thoughts spun out of control as blackness began to invade her.

The blackness of death.

RUGER KNEW by the time he reached Sarah, she could be dead.

If Bryce saw him coming, the man could simply hold her under longer. Ruger wouldn't be able to get to him in time.

His stomach clenched.

He couldn't let that happen.

That meant he would need to choose his next move very wisely.

Ruger hid behind the trees until he reached the lake. Bryce was probably twenty yards out, up to his chest.

How long had she been under now?

Too long.

Ruger knew he couldn't wait any longer.

He stepped out.

When Bryce saw him, he jerked Sarah from the water and grabbed a gun from under his shirt. The barrel went to Sarah's head as she emerged.

She sucked in air before sputtering.

She began coughing, almost violently.

The only reason she was upright was because Bryce had hold of her hair.

Anger rushed through Ruger as he stepped closer. "Let her go."

"You can't tell me what to do." A touch of glee filled Bryce's voice.

He was enjoying this, Ruger realized.

Sarah let out a cry as Bryce pressed the gun into her temple.

This man would pull the trigger.

Ruger had no doubt about that.

"If you kill her, I'm just going to kill you." Ruger drew his own gun.

As Bryce pushed her underwater again, he turned back to Ruger. "In that case, I'm going to have to kill you both."

He aimed the gun at Ruger.

Then he pulled the trigger.

Sarah couldn't let things end this way. Couldn't let Ruger die.

Was there anything she could do?

She needed to act quickly.

She'd already lost feeling in her feet, her hands. Her thoughts were becoming blurry.

But right now, Bryce was distracted by Ruger.

She might be able to use that to her advantage.

As Bryce plunged her back below the cold water, Sarah opened her eyes again and glanced around.

She raised both of her feet and shoved them into his chest. The water made the movement less effective, but Bryce lost some of his grip.

As he did, Sarah pushed herself away from him and emerged from the water.

When Bryce saw her, he growled with anger and lunged at her.

But this time, she dove under the water.

If he was going to kill her, she wasn't going to make it easy for him.

CHAPTER
FORTY-SIX

THE BULLET MISSED RUGER.

But he knew he couldn't wait any longer to help Sarah. He shoved his gun into his waistband then he dove into the water.

Sarah might be okay right now, but soon this water would claim her.

He needed to find her first.

As he surfaced to gulp in some air, he spotted Sarah treading water in the distance.

He started to dive back under to reach her when a hand clamped down on his ankle.

Bryce.

Ruger kicked away, quickly diving back under the water. He kept swimming until he reached Sarah.

His arms circled her waist. He lifted her, helping her stay afloat.

As his head emerged from the water, he glanced around.

Where was Bryce?

The man had disappeared.

Where had he gone?

As Sarah coughed, he rested her head on his shoulder.

"It's okay. You're okay."

He remained on guard, glancing around with trepidation.

Bryce was still nowhere in sight.

Quickly, he began swimming to the shore with Sarah. She was running out of time. Serious hypothermia could kick in at any moment.

He dragged her toward the shallow water. As he touched the bottom, he looked around again.

Bryce was back.

The man stood on a boulder at the water's edge, dripping wet and holding his gun.

Ignoring him, Ruger lifted Sarah from the water and began to walk to the shore.

"Don't take another step," Bryce growled, his gun outstretched.

Sarah moaned in his arms, shivers overtaking her.

Ruger couldn't just stand here with her. The temperature was in the fifties, and she was soaking wet.

"You need to put your gun down," Ruger said, still walking toward dry land.

If he stopped to grab his own gun, that would mean putting Sarah back into the water.

He couldn't do that.

"I don't think you have much say so right now," Bryce muttered. He scrambled from the rock and began walking toward them, his gun still outstretched.

"You don't want to do this." Ruger knew his words were probably meaningless.

He only hoped backup arrived soon.

"Don't tell me what I want to do. Now, I said stop walking!"

Ruger took another step, the water only to his ankles now. He set Sarah on her feet and pushed her behind him.

He would still help her to dry land. But, right now, he needed to put himself between her and Bryce.

She clung to his waist, unsteady, as Bryce continued to creep closer.

Ruger wanted to reach for his gun.

But he knew he couldn't risk it.

"I can't stop walking," he told Bryce, not liking how close the man was getting. "Sarah needs help."

"You're right. She does need help. A lot of help.

Help that only I can give her. Now take your hands off my wife!"

Sarah let out a soft gasp behind him.

"He's out of his mind, Ruger," she whispered. "Be careful."

She was talking. That was a good sign.

"You know you don't want to kill her with a bullet," Ruger said, the words paining him to say. "That would be too easy."

"No, I don't want to kill her with a bullet. I want to kill you that way."

The next instant, a blast filled the air.

Something sliced into his skin.

Pain erupted. Blood gushed.

He'd been shot.

Sarah heard the bullet whizzing through the air. Heard Ruger grunt. Saw the blood appear on his shoulder.

Her eyes widened.

Bryce had shot Ruger.

She glanced back at Bryce as he stood several feet away.

His eyes looked dazed, almost as if he hadn't expected to actually pull the trigger and hit someone.

But his gaze . . . it also showed just how off-balance he was.

She could see the signs of hypothermia setting in as well. His lips were blue. His skin pale.

He wouldn't be able to stay out in the cold much longer. Not soaking wet.

Bryce raised his gun and glanced at it, an almost crazy-looking smile on his face. "What do you know? Guns do work after they've been in the water."

Ruger pushed Sarah farther behind him. Despite the blood, he still appeared to be sharp and in control.

Bryce took another step toward them. "Why would you even want to be with someone like her? She's what we in the medical field like to call Looney Tunes. Of course, we never say that to the faces of our patients, only behind their backs."

Shame washed through her. But she pushed it away.

She had nothing to feel ashamed about.

Bryce was the one with issues. He'd abused her. Devalued her. He'd caused her untold misery. And she wouldn't allow him to manipulate her thoughts any longer.

"You didn't win, Bryce. No matter what you do. You can't control me anymore. Nothing you say or do will change that."

"You're wrong. You're weak. Pathetic."

Ruger spoke up, "Don't talk to her like that."

"I'll talk about her however I please. She's *my* wife."

"From what I understand, you remarried. She's no longer your wife. She's no longer yours, and she never will be again." Ruger's back seemed to broaden as Bryce crept closer with his gun.

Bryce scowled, a cocky look in his gaze. "You don't know what you're talking about."

"I know you should pick on someone your own size."

Bryce was about to give another comeback when Ruger seemed to see an opportunity.

He jerked his arm back. With one hand, he grabbed Bryce's gun. With the other, his fist collided with Bryce's jaw.

Bryce stood dazed a moment before collapsing into the shallow water of the lake. His mouth and nose remained above the waterline, ensuring he wouldn't drown.

Sarah was tempted to turn his head. To hold him under. To do to him what he'd done to her.

But she wouldn't sink to his level.

God was the ultimate judge, and Bryce would pay for his sins one day.

Besides, drowning wasn't a fitting punishment. Bryce deserved something that would humiliate him.

A public trial and years in prison would do that.

He continued to lie there unmoving, clearly unconscious.

They were safe.

For now.

Sarah turned toward Ruger, her teeth chattering as she observed him. This man had just risked his life for her. Had been shot while protecting her.

"You took a bullet for me . . ." she muttered.

"I took one for the president. Of course, I'd take one for you."

She flushed at his words. For so long, she didn't think she was worthy enough that someone would risk their own life for her. Bryce had made her feel like she wasn't valuable.

Ruger had changed that.

Sarah was almost more thankful for that than she was for the fact that Ruger had saved her life. Realizing your own worth was an entirely different way —a crucial way—of saving yourself.

Her gaze went to his shoulder, and she started to touch his wound but pulled back. "You're bleeding."

He glanced at his shoulder. "I'll be okay."

She threw her arms around him—on his uninjured side—and buried herself in the crook of his neck. "Thank you. You've given me my life back."

A noise in the distance caught her ear, and she looked over in time to see several vehicles zooming onto her property.

The police were here, she realized.

Ruger began leading her from the water.

Maybe this whole nightmare was finally over.

FORTY-SEVEN

AS PARAMEDICS TREATED HIS WOUND—THE bullet had just skimmed his shoulder—Ruger watched as Bryce was handcuffed and led away by the police.

Good. He hoped that man spent a long time behind bars.

His gaze wandered across the property to where Sarah sat in the back of an ambulance, a blanket around her.

She was safe.

She was healing.

She was free.

And he couldn't be more thankful.

Meanwhile, Jesse and Mateo had—with the permission of law enforcement—put wood over the cabin's broken window and fixed the front door.

After being cleared by the police, they left one of their vehicles for Ruger to drive until he got his SUV back. They headed back to Arizona to help with matters at the ranch. They were no longer needed here.

Detective Jefferson approached him and frowned. "I guess I owe you an apology."

"That's not necessary."

"I beg to differ. Ms. Chamberlain wouldn't be alive right now if it wasn't for you. I should have taken your claims more seriously."

"Bryce was the one who killed Clayton. He paid him off to switch out the drugs. Then he killed him in order to keep him silent, and he planted the murder weapon in my SUV."

The detective nodded. "I can see that now. I have no doubt the man will be going away for a long time, especially in light of Ms. Chamberlain's testimony."

"Good. That's what I want to hear."

Jesse had located Pierce. He'd been working at his practice all day.

The man was annoying and overzealous. But he wasn't guilty of any crimes.

Ruger glanced at Sarah. "Are you taking her to the hospital?"

"She's insisting that she's fine."

Ruger nodded. Even with Bryce in custody, he

figured Sarah probably still felt anxious being around doctors. That was to be expected.

The paramedic finished stitching him up. He didn't need to go to the hospital either.

He had more important matters to attend to.

Matters like Sarah.

"You mind coming to the station to give an official statement?" Detective Jefferson asked.

"Of course not." He glanced at Sarah. He would love a moment alone with her. But that was going to have to wait. "Can I make a phone call first?"

"Go ahead."

As the detective walked away, Ruger called Charlie and gave her the update.

This assignment was officially done.

Now he just had to find out what Sarah wanted to do next.

Stay here? Or start somewhere fresh?

Two hours later, Ruger and Sarah headed back to her place.

The two didn't say much on the drive.

Sarah figured it could all wait until they got inside.

But a surprising anxiety churned in her gut.

Would Ruger grab his bags and leave, assignment over?

The thought caused an ache to form in her heart.

So, she didn't bring it up on the drive.

She would wait.

Back at her house, she stepped inside and glanced around.

The guys had done a good job cleaning it up. Knowing Bryce had been inside wasn't comforting. But now that he was locked up, she hoped to move past that.

She paused in her kitchen and turned to Ruger, her heart pounding as she anticipated what this conversation might bring.

"Thank you for everything you did for me." Her throat burned as she said the words.

He stood in front of her, hands casually draped in the pockets of his jeans.

Did he feel any of the same nerves she did? Or was he unaffected by all of this?

"Of course. I would do it all over again if I had the choice."

She cleared her throat before asking the next question. "What's next for you? I assume you'll be going back to Vanishing Ranch."

"Maybe." He shrugged as if uncertain.

Or was that reluctance? Sarah wasn't sure.

"The good news for you is that you don't have to relocate unless you want to," he continued. "Bryce won't be hurting you again. According to Charlie, Bryce's current wife—Marsha—is going to press charges also. I have a feeling Bryce is going away for a very long time."

Her throat tightened at his words. "That's good to hear."

He waited quietly, questions in his gaze.

Even though the two of them hadn't known each other that long, it seemed too soon for Ruger to leave. But she was thankful that she could finally live in peace.

She did, however, have some decisions to make.

Should she stay here? Go back to St. Louis? Go somewhere fresh? Take back her old name or keep her current one?

Her head pounded as she looked up at Ruger and asked, "Are you leaving tonight?"

"It's a little late to leave, don't you think?"

"I do."

She swallowed hard as she felt the tension stretching between them.

He stared back at her.

As if operating in sync, Ruger reached for her waist. Sarah reached for his neck.

"You're not officially a client anymore," he muttered.

"I'm not, am I?"

The next instant, their lips met. The desire that had been building between them released as the kiss deepened.

Even when they pulled away, Sarah still felt herself clinging to him.

This felt too much like a goodbye.

She gazed up at him as she said, "I wish you could stay."

"You could come with me." He stared deeply into her eyes.

"To Vanishing Ranch?" Surprise rushed through her.

He nodded. "We can find something for you to do there."

Sarah's thoughts raced. She was touched at his offer, but she had to be honest with herself and him. "I can't see myself living there. I feel like my life is here now."

A frown tugged at his lips, but he nodded. "I understand. But I want to see you again. As often as I can."

A slow grin spread over her face. "I would like that. Maybe . . . I could visit Vanishing Ranch sometime."

A smile tugged at his lips. "We are going to figure this out."

Something about his words sounded so reassuring.

Sarah had learned life wasn't meant to be done alone. Yet that was exactly what she'd been doing for too long now. She'd been too afraid to get close to anyone.

But what was life without someone to share it with?

As she gazed up at Ruger, she hoped that someone would be him.

EPILOGUE
TWO MONTHS LATER

RUGER STRAIGHTENED when he saw the car coming through the gate of Vanishing Ranch.

He knew exactly who was inside.

Sarah.

She'd chosen to keep her new name.

A moment later, the vehicle stopped in front of him, and Sarah popped out.

She threw her arms around his neck.

Warmth filled him as he wrapped his arms around her waist and pulled her close.

"I'm so glad to see you," he whispered.

She stepped back and grinned. "I'm glad to see you too."

It had been three weeks since they'd last been together, and Ruger had gone up to Montana then.

They'd been doing the long-distance thing for a while now, and it seemed to be working.

Ruger knew that Sarah staying there was the right choice. She was establishing her life and her independence. It was important that she knew she could do that without a man nearby.

That was the same reason he hadn't insisted on picking her up and bringing her here. He never wanted her to feel controlled again.

But he missed her terribly when they were apart.

She glanced around and let out a sigh. "It's been a long time since I've been to this place."

"I'm sorry you ever had to come here at all."

She cast him a soft smile. "I never would have met you if I hadn't."

So much had happened since his time in Kalispell.

Bryce was in jail awaiting trial.

He'd been behind everything. And Ruger was right when he'd assumed someone was messing with Sarah's internet connection. That's how Bryce—or the guy he'd hired—had managed to circumvent the security system.

Bryce had arrived in the Flathead Lake area just in time to permanently silence Clayton and see to it himself that Sarah "got what was coming to her."

He'd denied all that to the police and acted like he

was the victim, that Sarah had tormented him. But no one was buying his lies.

And even though Detective Jefferson knew about Sarah's past now, he'd promised to remain quiet about it. He'd said if she ever needed anything that she could call him personally.

While here at the ranch, Ruger had also been busy looking into Benjamin Soldier's death. He'd used his connections to talk to several people.

They didn't have any answers yet, but he was moving closer. And he felt certain President Radar and his friend Jack Earl knew more than they were letting on. Was that because the information was classified? Or was there another reason?

He reached out his hand to Sarah. "Would you like to stretch your legs before dinner? Meet some of our newest horses?"

"I'd love to."

Hand in hand, he led her around the place.

It was early December here in Arizona, and the air was considerably cooler now than it was in the summer. The colors of the desert were beautiful and remarkable, and Vanishing Ranch was an amazing oasis in the middle of the otherwise barren land.

"You're doing good work here, Ruger," Sarah said as they paused near the mess hall.

"Thanks. I like to think so." His schedule had been busy as more and more cases came their way.

But he didn't ever want to get so wrapped up in his profession that he didn't take time for his personal life.

He wouldn't make the same mistakes now that he'd made with Khya.

"So . . . I've been talking to Charlie," he started.

Sarah raised her eyebrows. "Okay . . ."

"She agreed that it would help to have some of her guys established in different parts of the country so they can be ready to act as needed."

Sarah waited for him to continue.

His heart beat harder as his nerves kicked in. "After the new year, I was thinking about splitting my time between here and—"

"Montana?" she finished, almost looking breathless.

He nodded as he stared into her eyes, carefully watching her expression. "Yes. Montana. I was wondering what you thought about that."

"I think that's a wonderful idea."

A grin spread across his face. "I was hoping you might say that."

"In fact, I know of the perfect place. I think Kalispell is a beautiful area. The scenery is amazing."

"I was thinking that also."

Sarah's grin slipped as her gaze turned serious. "Ruger, I would love nothing more than for you to be close. But I don't want you giving up anything on my account—"

"I wouldn't be giving up anything—not if it means being in your life. I'd be gaining so much more."

She stared at him, her gaze misting. "Do you really mean that?"

"Completely. I can't have my entire life be my work. I can still do what I'm doing here but while up in Montana. There will just be stretches where I'll need to be gone—"

"I can work with that."

His head dipped down, and he continued to study her expression. "I know you've established your own life there. I don't want to impose on it."

"Are you kidding? I've dreamed about the day when we might actually live in the same state. Preferably the same town. Maybe even the same neighborhood."

Relief washed through him. "I would very much like that also."

He planted a kiss on her lips. Then a second one. Then a third.

Finally, he forced himself to pull away. There would be time for more later.

Right now, there were people who wanted to see Sarah.

But first, he had one more thing he wanted to talk to Sarah about.

"So . . . I have a friend who's a pilot," he started.

She squinted with curiosity. "Okay . . ."

"He agreed that, if you felt up to it, he'd fly us out to see your brother and his family."

Her eyes widened. "Really?"

Joy filled him. "Really."

She threw her arms around him. "I would love that. Thank you!"

He chuckled as he held her close. He was hoping that would be her reaction.

He knew how much her brother meant to her. Sarah deserved all the joy in the world—and he would give her whatever he could.

"For now, we should probably head inside," he murmured. "We can continue making these plans later. But Charlie had a special dinner prepared for you."

"She did? That sounds fantastic."

Ruger took her hand and led her inside, thankful for a second chance—for both of them.

~~~

Thank you for reading *Deadly Intent*. If you enjoyed this book, please consider leaving a review.

Keep reading for a preview of *Lethal Betrayal*.
~~~

CHRISTY BARRITT

Lethal BETRAYAL

VANISHING RANCH  THE SERIES – BOOK FIVE

LETHAL BETRAYAL: CHAPTER ONE

The sweltering landscape blurred around Emily Holcomb as she staggered forward.

"Keep moving," she murmured to herself. "You've got to keep moving."

She took another step, the motion taking entirely more energy than it should.

As despair began to set in, she licked her dry lips and sang, "Ain't no grave can hold my body down."

She sounded delirious, even to her own ears. But singing always helped calm her.

It reminded her of her determination not to let this desert be her grave—no matter how hard it tried.

Her granddad had loved the old gospel song. For some reason, the lyrics—as well as the memory of her grandad's deep voice as he sang it—brought her comfort and strength now.

Emily paused long enough to suck in a deep breath. Her heart pounded entirely too quickly, and she was hyper-aware of her pulse.

Finding a burst of strength, Emily pulled herself upright and surveyed the area. All she saw in every direction was a sun-bathed, parched desert.

Emily had been walking for hours, and she'd seen the same thing mile after mile. She thought maybe she would've reached one of the mountain ranges surrounding the area by now.

But she hadn't.

She was beginning to doubt she ever would.

Drawing in a breath, she forced herself to walk again. Her swirling head indicated she might fall forward at any minute.

But not if she could help it.

The sun continued to beat down on her. It had to be at least in the high nineties, which seemed unseasonably warm for the desert in October. However, the southwestern part of the United States was experiencing an unprecedented heat wave.

Was that where Emily was? It made the most sense.

But she wasn't sure. She'd been abducted in Los Angeles and had awoken in a strange place she didn't recognize. When she'd seen the opportunity to escape, she'd simply run. Her location made no difference—she only wanted to get away.

Kyle's image flashed in her mind, and Emily sneered.

Anger over the injustice of it all mixed with her fear.

She couldn't give up. First, she needed to bring down those men who preyed on the innocent, who loved wealth more than people.

That was exactly why those men wanted to control her—both out of vengeance for what she'd already done and out of desperation to stop her from ruining any more of their plans.

As Emily's resolve strengthened, she glanced forward.

Something ahead caught her eye, and she squinted.

Was that a . . . person?

Emily blinked and rubbed her eyes.

It almost looked like a man on horseback.

Or was he a desert mirage? Was she seeing things that simply weren't real?

She started to raise her hand and flag him down.

Then another thought hit her: What if that man worked for Arrow?

She froze as panic filled her.

As she turned to run, her head swirled.

She tumbled to the ground and blackness overtook her.

Mateo Garcia nudged The Lone Ranger—his black Arabian steed—with the side of his boot as they trotted through the desert. Bouncing over the landscape, his thoughts wandered to the photo he'd gotten via text yesterday.

A photo of his wife.

His deceased wife.

No words had been attached to the image. Just a haunting surveillance-like photo of his beautiful wife as she'd walked down the street of their small Mexican town. Mateo didn't know when or where the picture was taken.

He was only certain the photo had been snapped before she'd been abducted.

Before everything had changed.

Before his life had fallen apart and his heart had been crushed.

Why would someone send Mateo a picture of Rose?

Why now?

Unless the men who'd killed her were out for

blood and it was their way of signaling the coming trouble.

He'd have to figure that out later. For now, he shifted his thoughts back to the present.

More than one resident at Vanishing Ranch had reported seeing people wandering the desert near their property. Most likely, the wanderers were just adventure-seekers exploring the area.

But Mateo had to guard the people residing at the ranch. That meant he and his team had to make sure no strangers—or even worse, enemies—stumbled upon their location. Charlie Soldier, who owned and operated the ranch, had sensors to alert them whenever anyone got too close.

Mateo was mostly doing this out of an abundance of caution.

He continued to trot around the perimeter of the property, ignoring the vultures circling to the east. Something must have died out there. The desert was merciless in so many ways.

Despite the unseasonably hot day, he had to admit it was nice to be out here. He'd always loved horseback riding, and this area reminded him so much of the horse farm in Mexico where he'd grown up.

He'd lived in the United States for the past two years, and Arizona was beginning to feel like home.

He'd known he had to leave Mexico if he truly wanted to heal.

So that's what he'd done.

Something in the distance caught his attention. He pulled the binoculars from his belt and pressed them against his eyes.

He squinted.

What *was* that?

As Mateo got closer to the object, his back muscles tightened.

Was that a . . . person?

"*Vamos!*" He nudged The Lone Ranger to go faster.

His horse burst into a gallop.

The closer they got, the more Mateo's fears were confirmed.

This was . . . a woman.

A woman with curly dark hair, sunburnt skin, and wearing a flowered, knee-length sundress.

Mateo pulled back on the reins, signaling his horse to stop. Then he climbed off and rushed toward her.

Grabbing her shoulders, Mateo shifted her body until her face appeared. Her eyes were closed, her olive skin tinted red from sun exposure, and her lips chapped. Then there were the bruises on her cheek and around one eye. A cut stretched near her chin and another on her forehead.

And her dress . . . it had blood on it. A *lot* of blood.

He quickly checked her pulse and felt a beat.

Her eyes fluttered open a moment.

"Please . . . no . . ." She thrashed on the ground as her words slurred. "I . . . I can't go back there. Don't take me back."

"Take you back where? I'm not going to hurt you."

"Don't let them find me!"

The outburst lasted only a moment before she drifted back into unconsciousness.

Alarmed, Mateo stood and scanned the area. He didn't see anyone.

But that didn't mean no one was near.

Mateo grabbed his phone and called his leader at Vanishing Ranch. He needed a UTV out here.

This woman needed help.

Now.

Click Here to Keep Reading!

ALSO BY CHRISTY BARRITT:

a united effort to stop this killer before someone else dies.

Necessary Risk

When former Navy SEAL Hudson Carmichael sets out to rescue a woman in danger and bring her to Vanishing Ranch for refuge, he knows exactly what he needs to do. But his plan is thrown off course when he comes face-to-face with his dead fiancée. When Teagan Murphy unwillingly became entangled in the Farino crime family, she had no choice but to leave Hudson—and her entire life—behind. Now, as the stakes are raised, Teagan must find a way to disappear . . . again. She never expects Hudson, the only man she's ever loved, to be the one to rescue her. But he's here, and he has questions that need answers. As Hudson and Teagan work together to gain her freedom, they once again find themselves hoping for what might have been. But one secret is keeping Teagan alive—a secret that has the power to change everything.

Risky Ambition

Former Navy fighter pilot Nate Casper, also known as Ghost, splits his time between flying jet-setting celebrities around the world and volunteering to help with rescues at Vanishing Ranch. When movie star Chesney Blake books a trip with him, Ghost sets aside his attraction to her in order to remain professional. But when his flight plan gets waylaid by a barrage of bullets, putting Chesney in danger, his intention of keeping his distance takes a nosedive. Chesney Blake needs a break before filming her next movie. But when her getaway erupts into nothing short of chaos and her pilot transforms into her protector, her vacation plans are forgotten. Does someone really want her dead? Or was she even the intended target? As more incidents threaten their safety, Chesney and Ghost set out to uncover the truth. But as they get closer to finding answers, Chesney is faced with a fate worse than she ever imagined—even worse than death itself.

YOU ALSO MIGHT ENJOY: SALTWATER COWBOYS

Saltwater Cowboy

He's trying to forget. She'd give anything to remember. Officer Levi Sutherland wants to protect the wild horses of Cape Corral and keep the island residents safe. But memories of his deceased wife haunt him at every turn and make him long for a fresh start. When a woman washes ashore with a bullet wound and no memories, Levi knows he can't leave until he discovers what happened to her. The woman—whose necklace reads Dani—captures Levi's attention like no one has in a long time. But which side of the law is she on? Could Dani be mixed up with other mysterious incidents happening on the island? Together, can the two find answers and create new memories? Or will secrets tear them apart and destroy a future as uncertain as Dani's past?

Breakwater Protector

One secret will tear them apart. The other will pull them closer. Lizzie McCreary needs to disappear. As danger stalks her, she escapes to windswept Cape Corral with her eight-year-old son, Preston. The isolated island offers her a desperate hope for safety. Saltwater cowboy Dash Fulton isn't looking for love. Yet when he rescues a woman and boy from the woods, he immediately feels a bond with the two. He can sense the pair are harboring secrets. The question is, what are they? Dash has secrets of his own, and pressure continues to mount for him to come clean. But as he's caught up in the peril surrounding Lizzie and Preston, his own problems become a low priority. He can't let anyone hurt the sweet single mom and her precocious son. As more details come to light, will wounds from the past ultimately drive Lizzie and Dash apart? Or will the man chasing Lizzie destroy any hope for the future?

Cape Corral Keeper

They agreed to marry. But they never agreed to fall in love. When Cape Corral Fire Chief Dillon McGrath saves a woman wearing a wedding dress from drowning, he knows he'll have a great story to tell the guys at the station later. He never expected to get personally involved in the woman's plight to stay alive. Gracie Loveland had no choice but to run only moments before saying "I do" to her manipulative fiancé. Staying would have ultimately meant her death at the hands of the cruel man. Desperation, along with a dormant feistiness, surfaces as she fights to survive. Only one plan might keep Gracie safe and help Dillon preserve the island's wild horses. The idea seems crazy, but Dillon and Gracie can think of no other options. However, a foe from Gracie's past is closing in, determined to get what he wants regardless of whose life he destroys in the process.

Seagrass Secrets

He's her best friend. She's the woman of his dreams. Firefighter Colby Morris needs answers. After discovering a dead body, he then learns his best friend's address was in the man's pocket. He'll do anything to keep Emmy safe—yet he wants to keep his heart safe also. That's why he's never told Emmy he's in love with her. Emmy Sutherland is trying to make amends after she hits a man with her truck while driving in a torrential downpour. When the island's clinic floods, she has no choice but to let the stranger stay at her inn. But recent events on Cape Corral have her feeling apprehensive. Events continue to escalate, leaving Colby and Emmy scrambling to find answers. But as more secrets are uncovered, more danger arises. Can Colby and Emmy discover the truth? Or will their feelings get in the way—endangering not only their lives but their lifelong friendship?

Driftwood Danger

He's on one side of the fight to preserve Cape Corral. She's on the other. Abigail Ferguson wakes up in a strange place with bruises on her face and her hands bound. Someone is trying to teach her family a painful lesson and using Abigail as a pawn. When she's able to call for help, only one person comes to mind—law enforcement officer Grant Matthews. Grant has been crazy about Abigail since they met. But her wealthy family is a long-standing enemy of locals, and dating her would feel like a betrayal to the community he serves. However, when Abigail is abducted and needs his help, nothing will stop him from rescuing and protecting her. As Abigail's captor makes it clear he has more dastardly deeds planned, Grant and Abigail work together to try to find answers. But their growing feelings—and the obstacles between them—might put Abigail in even more danger. Can the two figure out this man's identity before it's too late? Or will the clever madman taunting Abigail stop at nothing to achieve what he wants?

ABOUT THE AUTHOR

USA Today has called Christy Barritt's books "scary, funny, passionate, and quirky."

Christy writes both mystery and romantic suspense novels that are clean with underlying messages of faith. Her books have sold more than three million copies and have won the Daphne du Maurier Award for Excellence in Suspense and Mystery, have been twice nominated for the Romantic Times Reviewers' Choice Award, and have finaled for both a Carol Award and Foreword Magazine's Book of the Year.

She is married to her Prince Charming, a man who thinks she's hilarious—but only when she's not trying to be. Christy is a self-proclaimed klutz, an avid music lover who's known for spontaneously bursting into song, and a road trip aficionado.

When she's not working or spending time with her family, she enjoys singing, playing the guitar, and exploring small, unsuspecting towns where people have no idea how accident-prone she is.

Find Christy online at:
www.christybarritt.com
www.facebook.com/christybarritt
www.twitter.com/cbarritt

Sign up for Christy's newsletter to get information on all of her latest releases here: **www.christybarritt. com/newsletter-sign-up/**

COMPLETE BOOK LIST

Squeaky Clean Mysteries:

- #1 Hazardous Duty
- #2 Suspicious Minds
- #2.5 It Came Upon a Midnight Crime (novella)
- #3 Organized Grime
- #4 Dirty Deeds
- #5 The Scum of All Fears
- #6 To Love, Honor and Perish
- #7 Mucky Streak
- #8 Foul Play
- #9 Broom & Gloom
- #10 Dust and Obey
- #11 Thrill Squeaker
- #11.5 Swept Away (novella)
- #12 Cunning Attractions
- #13 Cold Case: Clean Getaway

#14 Cold Case: Clean Sweep

#15 Cold Case: Clean Break

#16 Cleans to an End

While You Were Sweeping, A Riley Thomas Spinoff

The Sierra Files:

#1 Pounced

#2 Hunted

#3 Pranced

#4 Rattled

The Gabby St. Claire Diaries (a Tween Mystery series):

The Curtain Call Caper

The Disappearing Dog Dilemma

The Bungled Bike Burglaries

The Worst Detective Ever

#1 Ready to Fumble

#2 Reign of Error

#3 Safety in Blunders

#4 Join the Flub

#5 Blooper Freak

#6 Flaw Abiding Citizen

#7 Gaffe Out Loud

#8 Joke and Dagger

#9 Wreck the Halls

#10 Glitch and Famous

Raven Remington

Relentless

Holly Anna Paladin Mysteries:

#1 Random Acts of Murder

#2 Random Acts of Deceit

#2.5 Random Acts of Scrooge

#3 Random Acts of Malice

#4 Random Acts of Greed

#5 Random Acts of Fraud

#6 Random Acts of Outrage

#7 Random Acts of Iniquity

Lantern Beach Mysteries

#1 Hidden Currents

#2 Flood Watch

#3 Storm Surge

#4 Dangerous Waters

#5 Perilous Riptide

#6 Deadly Undertow

Lantern Beach Romantic Suspense

Tides of Deception

Shadow of Intrigue

Storm of Doubt

Winds of Danger

Rains of Remorse

Torrents of Fear

Lantern Beach P.D.

On the Lookout

Attempt to Locate

First Degree Murder

Dead on Arrival

Plan of Action

Lantern Beach Escape

Afterglow (a novelette)

Lantern Beach Blackout

Dark Water

Safe Harbor

Ripple Effect

Rising Tide

Lantern Beach Guardians

Hide and Seek

Shock and Awe

Safe and Sound

Lantern Beach Blackout: The New Recruits

Rocco

Axel

Beckett

Gabe

Lantern Beach Mayday

Run Aground

Dead Reckoning

Tipping Point

Lantern Beach Blackout: Danger Rising

Brandon

Dylan

Maddox

Titus

Lantern Beach Christmas

Silent Night

Crime á la Mode

Dead Man's Float

Milkshake Up

Bomb Pop Threat

Banana Split Personalities

Beach Bound Books and Beans Mysteries

Bound by Murder

Bound by Disaster

Vanishing Ranch

Forgotten Secrets

Necessary Risk

Risky Ambition

Deadly Intent

Lethal Betrayal (coming soon)

The Sidekick's Survival Guide

The Art of Eavesdropping

The Perks of Meddling

The Exercise of Interfering

The Practice of Prying

The Skill of Snooping

The Craft of Being Covert

Saltwater Cowboys

Saltwater Cowboy

Breakwater Protector

Cape Corral Keeper

Seagrass Secrets

Driftwood Danger

Unwavering Security

Beach House Mysteries

The Cottage on Ghost Lane

The Inn on Hanging Hill

The House on Dagger Point

School of Hard Rocks Mysteries

The Treble with Murder

Crime Strikes a Chord

Tone Death

Carolina Moon Series

Home Before Dark

Gone By Dark

Wait Until Dark

Light the Dark

Taken By Dark

Suburban Sleuth Mysteries:

Death of the Couch Potato's Wife

Fog Lake Suspense:

Edge of Peril

Margin of Error

Brink of Danger

Line of Duty

Legacy of Lies

Secrets of Shame

Refuge of Redemption

Cape Thomas Series:
Dubiosity
Disillusioned
Distorted

Standalone Romantic Mystery:
The Good Girl

Suspense:
Imperfect
The Wrecking

Sweet Christmas Novella:
Home to Chestnut Grove

Standalone Romantic-Suspense:
Keeping Guard
The Last Target
Race Against Time
Ricochet
Key Witness
Lifeline
High-Stakes Holiday Reunion
Desperate Measures
Hidden Agenda
Mountain Hideaway
Dark Harbor

Shadow of Suspicion

The Baby Assignment

The Cradle Conspiracy

Trained to Defend

Mountain Survival

Dangerous Mountain Rescue

Nonfiction:

Characters in the Kitchen

Changed: True Stories of Finding God through Christian Music (out of print)

The Novel in Me: The Beginner's Guide to Writing and Publishing a Novel (out of print)

www.ingramcontent.com/pod-product-compliance
Lightning Source LLC
Chambersburg PA
CBHW031439160726
47994CB00005B/1796